"Adrian, I can put up with all of this.

"I am willing to live in this marriage with nothing more from you than your polite regard. I am even willing to let go of my dreams of having a husband who loves me. But I will not lie beneath you and pretend that I am happy. I will not lie still in my bed and act as though I do not want more."

"You do not mind the liberties I took? You would welcome them?"

She could not admit to more embarrassing truths to him. She could not...

He lifted her chin and she thought she saw mirth glittering in his hazel-colored eyes. How could a woman not enjoy being naked with a man like this?

Miranda reached up and slid her fingers through his hair. Pulling his head down, she kissed him, tasting the brandy on his tongue and letting him taste her. Out of breath, she nodded to him in answer to the question that still circled inside her thoughts.

"I would welcome them, Adrian. I would."

He kissed her this time, and she grabbed the lapels of his evening coat to keep her balance...!

The Du
Harlequin

D1041179

Praise for Terri Brisbin

"A lavish historical romance in the grand
tradition from a wonderful talent."
—*New York Times* bestselling author
Bertrice Small on *Once Forbidden*

The Countess Bride
"Brisbin woos her readers with laughter and tears
in this delightful and interesting tale of love."
—*Romantic Times*

The Norman's Bride
"A quick-paced story with engaging characters
and a tender love story."
—*Romantic Times*

The Dumont Bride
"Rich in its Medieval setting…Terri Brisbin
has written an excellent tale that will keep you
warm on a winter's night."
—*Affaire de Coeur*

**DON'T MISS THESE OTHER
TITLES AVAILABLE NOW:**

#752 ROCKY MOUNTAIN MAN
Jillian Hart

#753 THE MISSING HEIR
Gail Ranstrom

#754 HER DEAREST ENEMY
Elizabeth Lane

The Duchess's Next Husband

TERRI BRISBIN

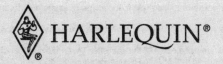

HARLEQUIN®

TORONTO • NEW YORK • LONDON
AMSTERDAM • PARIS • SYDNEY • HAMBURG
STOCKHOLM • ATHENS • TOKYO • MILAN • MADRID
PRAGUE • WARSAW • BUDAPEST • AUCKLAND

If you purchased this book without a cover you should be aware
that this book is stolen property. It was reported as "unsold and
destroyed" to the publisher, and neither the author nor the
publisher has received any payment for this "stripped book."

ISBN 0-373-29351-8

THE DUCHESS'S NEXT HUSBAND

Copyright © 2005 by Theresa S. Brisbin

All rights reserved. Except for use in any review, the reproduction or
utilization of this work in whole or in part in any form by any electronic,
mechanical or other means, now known or hereafter invented, including
xerography, photocopying and recording, or in any information storage
or retrieval system, is forbidden without the written permission of the
publisher, Harlequin Enterprises Limited, 225 Duncan Mill Road,
Don Mills, Ontario, Canada M3B 3K9.

All characters in this book have no existence outside the imagination of
the author and have no relation whatsoever to anyone bearing the same
name or names. They are not even distantly inspired by any individual
known or unknown to the author, and all incidents are pure invention.

This edition published by arrangement with Harlequin Books S.A.

® and TM are trademarks of the publisher. Trademarks indicated with
® are registered in the United States Patent and Trademark Office, the
Canadian Trade Marks Office and in other countries.

www.eHarlequin.com

Printed in U.S.A.

Available from Harlequin Historicals and
TERRI BRISBIN

Please address questions and book requests to:
Harlequin Reader Service
U.S.: 3010 Walden Ave., P.O. Box 1325, Buffalo, NY 14269
Canadian: P.O. Box 609, Fort Erie, Ont. L2A 5X3

To Mary Lou Frank, Susan Stevenson,
Jennifer Wagner Schmidt, Lyn Wagner,
Mary Stella and Colleen Admirand—
wonderful women, talented writers
and extraordinary friends and colleagues.
Thank you for being there through the
ups and downs and everywhere in between,
and especially for getting me through
2003 and 2004.
Huzzah!

Prologue

He slipped inside her body with a practiced ease from their many joinings. Although she softened beneath him, she gave no outward sign that she enjoyed this now as she had in the early days of their marriage. Judging from her reactions to his movements, it was most likely less now than then.

Adrian moved them efficiently toward completion and, even as she let out a soft sigh, he offered a silent prayer that this time they might be successful in creating the heir he needed so much. For the dukedom, he prayed, as he filled her once more and felt his seed begin to release. For his family name and honor, he urged silently, as he thrust deeper within her again. For the continuation of his name, he implored, to whatever power controlled these matters.

Without a word, he withdrew from his wife. Climbing from her bed, he tugged on his robe and ran his fingers through his hair. When he heard the telltale sound of her shifting, and the rustling of the bedcovers, he turned toward the bed and nodded.

"Thank you, my dear," he said. He always said the same thing, since he appreciated his wife's cooperation and efforts to gain an heir.

"Windmere," she replied softly, without ever meeting his gaze.

He nodded at her and returned to his dressing room. Within the hour, the Duke of Windmere was at his club enjoying a particularly good port. And he realized, as the butler served him without him saying a word, that his life was nothing if not predictable.

Chapter One

"Turn your head, if you please, Your Grace."

Adrian Warfield, Duke of Windmere, suffered the poking and prodding in silence. His name and position had brought three of England's leading physicians to his home, and his inbred manners prevented him from allowing the escape of the oaths he wanted to speak. If these three men could give him no answers, his future and that of his family and dukedom looked increasingly bleak. Allowing each of them in turn a chance to examine him, Adrian grew impatient when it seemed that the appointment dragged on for too long.

Finally, finally, they stepped away and he adjusted his shirt and waistcoat. Leaving the ends of his linen cravat hanging down on his chest, Adrian waited for their pronouncement. They stood in a cluster by his desk, whispering among themselves and glancing at him as they consulted on his condition.

"Well, Doctors. What is your diagnosis?" He liked none of the expressions that met his gaze. The silence grew until it made his skin itch, and he spat out one of the curses he'd held in until that moment. "Bloody hell! Just get on with it."

They looked to each other before facing him.

"Your Grace, we have nothing new to offer you regarding your condition," Dr. Penworthy said. His bushy eyebrows twitched, giving him a vaguely squirrel-like appearance.

"But it has worsened?" Adrian prepared himself for the worst.

"It has, Your Grace, but not so much that we are overly concerned by the changes you presented." Dr. Lloyd pulled out a small notebook and nodded at the desk. "An adjustment or two to the tonics you are using should be just the thing to deal with the symptoms."

Adrian stepped aside and allowed Dr. Lloyd to sit in his chair and write out instructions to the apothecary. Although Drs. Penworthy and Wilkins exchanged glances again, neither had any other recommendations and allowed Dr. Lloyd to speak for them.

"Your Grace, do not let these changes affect you so much. We know that a nervous personality will exacerbate your lung condition." All three nodded in agreement and Adrian scowled in response at each of them individually. Dr. Lloyd held out the paper to him with the scrawled instructions. "Take the waters a few times this summer and you will feel like a new man."

Closing his eyes for a moment, Adrian fought for control over his frustration. No need to give the impression that he had the nervous personality they'd spoken of. No need to let on that he would like to strangle them all. Anger pulsed within him, alive, potent and growing. With an astuteness that surprised him, the three older men met his gaze directly. They knew how helpless he felt in the face of his condition. And helpless was not how a man wanted to feel.

"We will see ourselves out, Your Grace," Dr. Wilkins said softly. "We are at your service if the need arises."

Adrian accepted their bows and watched wordlessly as they opened the door and left. Realizing that he was crumbling the paper in his fist, he smoothed it open and tossed it on his desk. Walking to the other end of his study, he looked out the window at the bright, clear day before him. Dropping into the high-backed chair near the window, he tried to release the tension that spiraled inside him. They were correct about that—allowing the anger and frustration free rein did increase the number and severity of the attacks.

Leaning his head back, he closed his eyes again and listened to the sounds outside his house. The clip-clop of horses. The rustling of the branches of the trees in the spring breeze. The gentle calls of birds. The doctors' voices.

The doctors' voices?

Adrian got to his feet and positioned himself next to

the open window where he could see and not be seen. The three doctors stood a few yards from him and, though they lowered their voices in a discreet fashion, he heard their every word.

"A terrible pity, really." Lloyd?

"And nothing to be done?" That was certainly Wilkins. Adrian shifted to hear better. Who were they discussing?

"And in the prime of his life. Sad case." He could almost picture Penworthy's eyebrows twitching as he spoke.

"Shouldn't he be told? I do worry about that," Lloyd admitted in a fretful voice. "There are preparations to be made, arrangements to be handled, and so many rely on his oversight and condescension."

An icy shiver slid down Adrian's back and he straightened away from the aperture. Beads of sweat gathered on his own brow and trickled down his face and neck. The room had not grown hotter. Fear, plain and clear, caused his body to react to the horrible news, a sense of foreboding that grew within him.

It could not be….

It simply could not be…him.

"With his titles and lands, all the crucial details are already handled." Penworthy continued, "A man with his status and responsibilities, and especially one with no heirs-of-his-body, has everything in order at all times. No, I think it best not to reveal the direness of his true situation."

There was a pause, as though they were considering Penworthy's recommendation to keep him unadvised of his perilous condition.

His condition?

He shook his head, trying to clear his thoughts, for he must be hearing their words incorrectly. They had just assured him to his face that he was only a slight bit worse. Change his decoctions. Take the waters. They'd not warned him of his impending death.

"How long, do you think?" Wilkins asked. "Such a marked deterioration cannot be a good sign."

"A half year? Perhaps through the winter? I cannot be more specific than that without an unacceptable amount of conjecture on my part," Lloyd declared. "We will watch his condition and do what we can to relieve his symptoms. Especially as they worsen."

They paused then and Adrian wiped the sweat from his face with the back of his hand. As their words began to sink into his mind, he shook his head again. It could not be. It simply could not be.

"That poor man," Penworthy said. "The noblest of blood cannot protect you once Death has you marked as his own."

A moment of silence was all they spared him then. The clattering of wheels on cobblestones and the familiar sound of Adrian's coachman calling out to his team told him that his carriage had pulled in front of the house to take them back to their respective offices. The vehicle rolled away down the street and he was left with the awful truth.

Adrian Warfield, Duke of Windmere, would be dead by the year's end.

Time had stopped for him, but his death sentence still echoed through the chamber. Stunned by the words spoken by his physicians, Adrian could not think rationally. Scattered thoughts and memories flooded his mind as he tried to grab on to something that would make sense of this insanity.

Long ago, when discussing with his older brother the bravery of soldiers facing death, he had thought in a fleeting way of how he would handle himself if ever in that situation. Now, the courage and daring spoken of then disappeared, and a raw, gut-wrenching fear tore at him, making his legs quiver and his stomach churn.

He did not know how long the inertia of shock held him prisoner in the chair, simply breathing in and out to keep the prophesy of his death at bay. Dust motes floated before him and the sounds of the street outside his windows faded away. Aware of only the growing turmoil within, he stared off into the distance and waited for it to hit.

And, like an unprovoked punch in the gut, it did.

As the news began to settle in, Adrian stumbled to the cabinet, grabbed the crystal decanter of port and lurched from his study. Ignoring the startled looks of his man-of-business and his butler, he strode to the stairs and climbed to the second floor, where his rooms were located. Bolting past his valet, he slammed the door and locked it behind him.

He put the port down on the table next to his bed and pulled his cravat from around his neck. Tugging at the buttons, he ripped his waistcoat off and then threw it across the room. Loosening his shirt, he tried to calm himself with a few deep breaths. The coughing spasms he feared were on him instantly and he doubled over from the strength of them.

Minutes went by as hours while the very breath was squeezed from his lungs, but finally he could feel the spasms lessen. Collapsing on his bed, he pulled air into his body, fighting not to lose consciousness. The banging on the door drew his attention and he heard his valet's loud whisper through the door.

"Your Grace? Your Grace?" Thompson's voice was filled with concern, a concern that Adrian did not want at this moment.

"Leave me be, Thompson. I am well," he called out.

Coughing again, he lay back on the bed's cool surface and waited for the attack to end. A few more spasms and a number of coughs and then it ceased. Adrian pushed himself up, shrugged off his waistcoat and reached for the port. In a move that he knew would horrify his servants and his wife if they ever witnessed it, he brought the decanter to his mouth and swallowed several mouthfuls of the fortified wine.

Leaning back against the mahogany headboard, he listened to the sounds of whispering outside his door.

Two—no, three—people were out there trying to decide what to do about him, and he guessed the group included Thompson, his valet, Sherman, his butler, and perhaps even Webb, his secretary and man-of-business, whose meeting had been cut short with the arrival of the physicians.

No matter. Adrian could not face them until he faced himself and accepted what the doctors had told him. And that called for the consumption of as much distilled spirits as he could handle. Or not handle. He looked at the bottle in his hand and wondered if there was enough port there for his needs. There was always the twenty-five-year-old whisky in the locked cabinet—that would more than meet his requirements.

Adrian lifted the bottle again to his mouth and drank deeply. The warmth settled his stomach and began to spread out to his limbs. Unable to face the reality of his all-too-short future, he decided to drink until the news was blotted from his thoughts.

Smiling grimly, he realized he would need to break into his late father's private stock for something stronger to deaden the shock of the news of his own impending demise. Facing death was not as easy as he had imagined all those years ago.

Chapter Two

Miranda Warfield, the Duchess of Windmere, stood silently while her maid opened her dressing room door. Allowing a final smoothing of fabric and tucking of loosened strands of hair by her maid, she hesitated for a moment. Then, setting her feet on the well-worn path down the hall, she began the walk that would lead from His Grace's room down to the dining room for a late supper.

Each of her days was filled with just such repetitive behavior. Rising from sleep, eating meals, dressing for engagements and going to sleep again all fit neatly into a narrowly defined schedule for the Duchess of Windmere. Pausing in front of her husband's door, she realized that since today was Thursday, the night would end with Windmere's weekly visit to her bed. And on the morrow, when faced with the dowager duchess's thinly disguised question about the condition of her health, at their ritual Friday morning breakfast, Miranda could smile demurely and simply nod, saying without words that she was doing her duty to the duke in all facets of their life.

She arrived at the duke's door and waited for his valet to open it. The slight pause expanded to several seconds and then to nearly a full minute. Startled by this change, she cocked her head and listened for any activity within. It was a regrettable habit from her past, but one that was useful at times. Loud whispers and scuffling feet were evident, but she did not hear His Grace's deep voice. She had just decided to knock when Fisk rushed to her side.

"Allow me, Your Grace," her efficient maid said, stepping around her and knocking on the door.

Miranda was reminded once more that she had servants to do her bidding and that something as innocuous as knocking on a door was beneath her now. Standing quietly as they awaited a response, she thought on how strange this was. It was at times like this that she longed to be the squire's daughter once more, with little or none of the pretense needed to live this life. Shaking her head, she banished the thoughts before they could take hold.

The door swung open and, instead of Windmere, Thompson the valet stepped forward. This, too, was very strange.

"Your Grace," he said as he bowed deeply to her.

"Thompson."

"His Grace will be unavailable to join you for dinner, but he bids you to enjoy your outings this evening." The strain in his voice told her that this was not usual. She swore his left eye was twitching as he spoke. Another sign of this upheaval in the normal decorum?

The two servants turned to her, obviously awaiting her reaction. Before she could speak, a loud crash and a string of rather earthy curses came from Windmere's bedchamber. Thompson coughed loudly, an obvious yet unsuccessful attempt to disguise the words not meant for a lady's ears. It was definitely Windmere's voice, but she had not heard it raised in anger, as it was now, for many years.

"Your pardon, Your Grace. His Grace is indisposed."

Decorum is more important than anything else in a duke or duchess's life.

The dowager's words rang in her thoughts, and Miranda knew what was expected of her. She nodded to Thompson and turned from the door. Walking down the hall and then down the stairs to the dining room, she was pleased that no one who watched her would be able to see the turmoil filling her thoughts as she contemplated her husband's remarkable condition.

She sat in the chair, held out by the butler, and realized that the last time she'd heard Windmere yelling in anger was before he'd ascended to the title, when he was still Adrian and she was only slightly less suitable for him as a second son. Since he'd become the duke, he never raised his voice to her or expressed anything other than polite enthusiasm during conversations or engagements. This was extraordinary.

The first dish was placed before her and she took no notice of what it was. How could she when something so different had drawn her attention? Sherman repeated its ingredients, but it could have been dirt laced with arsenic for all she heard. Slicing into it and lifting the fork to her mouth, Miranda finally realized what the true surprise was.

Her husband, the Duke of Windmere, was drunk.

The food in her mouth turned to dust as she took in this insight. He had never, not in all the years she'd known him, before or after their marriage, before or since accepting the title, been drunk in her presence or within her hearing. But he was now. Miranda took a sip of the wine in her goblet to ease the food's way.

"Is something wrong with the scallops, Your Grace?" Sherman leaned in closer to whisper the question to her. It would be unseemly if she were to complain too loudly.

"It is fine, Sherman. Please continue with the next course."

Drifting back to her thoughts over the duke's condition, she knew that he was extremely angry about something, angry enough to drink to excess. So angry that he was purposely breaking items in his chamber. What could have him so upset?

It is inappropriate and unacceptable for a wife to inquire about or to meddle in the affairs of her husband or his interests.

Miranda blinked as she heard once more the dowager's voice issuing another warning about her behavior. The words were as clear as if the woman sat at table with her. Miranda sat up straighter and tried to focus on the food being placed before her; that was surely something appropriate for her attention.

But the surprising behavior of the duke had rattled her. Not that he was drunk, for she knew men drank and sometimes drank to excess. Not that he was angry, although it was out of character with His Grace's deportment of the last several years.

No, what rattled her and made her thoughts drift into inappropriate directions was that, for the first time in such a very long time, their lives were not following the ritual and regimented schedule that had been established. For the first time, she had been surprised and a bit shocked, something that had not happened between her and her husband in too many years. For the first time in too long, the duke showed himself to be a simple man with faults and weaknesses.

Miranda shivered with a completely inappropriate measure of anticipation that there might be a real person existing within the shell of the duke. For one moment, she let herself remember the promising beginning to their marriage and to wish for a real life instead of this sham and ritual and politeness. Although she regretted whatever it was that caused the duke such upset, part of her was extremely pleased. There was life in Adrian, after all.

* * *

The morning dawned bright and clear, and the aroma of chocolate awakened her from her sleep. Sliding up in bed, she leaned against the cushions a maid arranged behind her, and watched as the morning tray of chocolate and toast was placed over her lap. Taking a sip of the thick, hot beverage, Miranda realized she still wore her dressing gown over her night rail.

Her husband had missed their weekly appointment!

In spite of his absence at dinner, she'd thought he would visit as usual, and so she'd gone to bed as she did every Thursday evening—in her night rail with her dressing gown on. Adrian would put out the bedside candle, slip under the covers, slide the gown from her shoulders and go about his business. When he'd left, she would go to her dressing room, wash, leave the gown at the foot of the bed and fall to sleep.

Shaking her head, she realized he'd not visited for the first time in months, years perhaps.

"Your Grace?" the maid whispered, curtsying as she approached the bedside. "Is something wrong with your chocolate? Should I bring you another cup?"

"No, Betsy," she replied, shaking her head on purpose this time. "Is His Grace…still…?"

"Indisposed, Your Grace?" The young maid added the correct polite term for her husband's condition last evening.

"Indisposed. Or has he left for his morning ride?"

Miranda shifted on the bed as she asked, and placed the porcelain cup back on the tray. "The weather certainly looks favorable for a ride in the park."

Did the maid comprehend her curiosity? Miranda tried to keep just the right tone of disinterest in her voice, but feared her underlying questions were being betrayed…to a maid.

Before Betsy could answer her questions, the door opened and Fisk stepped in. With a look at her first, her competent lady's maid dismissed the young girl with a nod and waited for Betsy to leave before speaking.

"His Grace is still abed and did not leave the house last night after he missed dinner."

"How very strange."

The words slipped out before she could stop them, but if Fisk thought them unusual or unseemly, she did not, would not, say so. It was amazing that the change in the duke's behavior for one evening could throw the whole household into disarray so easily.

Motioning that she was finished with the half-eaten toast and chocolate, Miranda waited for it to be removed and then slid from her bed. Walking into her dressing room, she found her clothes laid out and ready for her. Fisk stepped into the room and, with her usual efficiency, soon had Miranda dressed, with her hair arranged, and ready to face her weekly interview by the duke's mother.

As the door to her chambers was opened for her, Miranda realized she would never be ready to face this particular ritual in the Warfield family. At least not until she could bring the news that she carried Windmere's heir. And with each passing month and year, that declaration seemed more and more unlikely.

The drive to the dowager's residence a few blocks away did not take long enough for her to banish completely the questions that pushed forward into her thoughts. As she entered the drawing room and took a seat on the couch nearest the windows overlooking the gardens, she breathed deeply, trying to regain a sense of calm, a sense of her true self, before she was confronted by her dragonlike mother-by-marriage.

"Miranda."

At the very sound of the commanding voice, Miranda stood and nodded. One did not remain seated when Cordelia Masters Warfield, dowager Duchess of Windmere, entered a room. No matter whose precedence was higher. No matter the age of those waiting or their position in society. Everyone stood when Her Grace entered. Miranda had it on good authority that even the Regent himself reacted so in the dowager's presence.

With a posture and gait that any governess or tutor in the womanly arts would be proud of, the older woman crossed the expansive room to the large chair across from where Miranda had chosen to sit.

On another woman, the soft white of her hair and the clear blue gaze would have been inviting and warm. On the dowager, however, it only accented the harsh lines of dissatisfaction around her mouth and the coldness of that gaze.

Lowering herself to the seat, Cordelia placed herself exactly six inches from the back of the chair and laid her hands on her lap. Miranda knew it was six inches because Cordelia always reminded her of the correct posture and bearing needed by a duchess, whether in public or private.

Attempting to follow her example, Miranda sank to the couch, straightened her spine and crossed her own hands in her lap. When the dowager simply cleared her throat instead of coughing discreetly, Miranda knew she had attained the desired position. The cough was a signal to the butler to bring in the tea.

Arriving too late for a country breakfast and too early for a city one, Miranda knew not to expect more than the tea and biscuits placed before her. Cordelia hated city hours and was up at dawn, complaining liberally of the lack of fortitude in others who needed to sleep away most of their mornings. Having lived with this woman prior to her husband attaining his title, Miranda knew exactly what to expect. The dowager simply wanted a report, and then Miranda would be dismissed with as little regard as the servants were. Any pretenses of warmth and caring had dissipated as the hoped-for heir never appeared.

"How are you this morning, Miranda?" Although the dowager stirred her tea, her gaze never left Miranda's face. She was looking for signs…of a *delicate condition*.

"I am well, Your Grace. And you?" Miranda looked away, giving the answer without the words. Still barren. When she turned back, the grimace still tightened the older woman's face.

"My goddaughter will be attending Lady Crispin's ball next week. Do you plan on attending as well?"

The subject changed neatly from a distressingly personal one to an unremarkable social one, without so much as a moment's hesitation and without any acknowledgment of the woman's continued disappointment. Miranda simply nodded.

"And my son?"

"Your Grace, I would not presume to know Windmere's schedule." Cordelia's eyes narrowed as she looked for some sign of disrespect in her words. Miranda met her intense gaze with a guileless one. "I could ask His Grace's secretary if you wish me to?"

Miranda had aided Cordelia's attempts to launch her goddaughter in society, and she would continue to do so. She would not hold her own anger and frustration at the dowager against an innocent girl.

"I will send word to his secretary," Cordelia announced, standing and smoothing the elaborate morning gown as she did.

"About what, Mother?"

Miranda gave a start at the sound of her husband's voice. Turning slowly in her seat, she watched as Adrian walked into the drawing room and greeted his mother and her with a civilized nod. One look at his gait and the way he held his head told her that he was suffering the lingering effects of his condition the evening before.

"I would appreciate your presence at the Crispins' ball next week. It will only be Juliet's third one since •

her presentation to the queen and, as family, it is appropriate for us to attend with her." The dowager paused and passed her sharp gaze over her son.

"Are you well, Windmere?" She asked her question, but assessed her son even as she spoke. "You look rather washed out and peaked."

Miranda examined Adrian's appearance as well. His linen, like the rest of his garments, was immaculate as usual, and he was done up in the latest fashion. He'd recently had his longish hair clipped in a shorter style and it revealed the natural body of it as the black locks curled just above his collar. He still cut a dashing figure, as he had when they'd met, so long ago.

It was not his clothing that gave away his condition as much as the sallowness of his normally tanned complexion and the red streaks in the whites of his eyes. He looked every inch the man suffering from the aftermath of too much alcohol.

"I am fine, Mother. Just tired," he said. Meeting Miranda's gaze, he seemed to be waiting for her to reveal the truth. When she simply nodded, he continued, "I am not certain of my plans over these next few weeks. I must go to Windmere Park to deal with some…business, and I do not know when I will return."

He saw his wife's eyes narrow at his hesitation and waited for Miranda's questions. They did not come. But of course not. Miranda had been trained as the perfect lady by his mother, and would never question him in public. And since being under the dowager's tutelage, she did not question him in private, either.

How would she react to the news of her impending widowhood? Would she react at all? Now was not the time to present such information. First, Adrian knew, he must sort through the practicalities and legalities of what his death would cause, and then he would speak to her about it. Or mayhap the physicians had the right of it—better not to know too far ahead of such a dire circumstance?

"When Parliament is in session? I thought you were keen on speaking to some of the issues," his mother said. He could see that she definitely wanted to press him on this, but her unwavering control over something as trite as curiosity did not wane.

With her steely gaze on him, he tried to organize his thoughts in spite of the pounding in his head, the churning of his stomach and the stinging in his eyes. Dragging a hand through his hair, he took a deep breath before answering.

"There are estate concerns which I must resolve, Mother. I will miss only a few sessions while protecting our family's interests in the north." He played the trump card in his hand—family matters—ruthlessly.

Then, to his horror, a cough welled up deep inside his lungs. Walking to the door that opened to the gardens, and trying to appear nonchalant, he lifted his hand to his mouth to cover the worst of it. For once, Providence heard his plea and no more followed the first.

"Would you like me to accompany you?" Miranda's soft voice drew his attention, but he kept his back turned. "I have no pressing engagements here in town."

Had she any idea of how brandy-faced he'd been last evening? He remembered cursing his fate in rather loud and vulgar language…had she heard? With so many uncertainties ahead of him, Adrian decided he should make this trip alone.

"There is no reason for you to give up the Season at its height for the dull country, my dear. I shan't be away for more than a week at the most."

He faced her now and noticed the brightness of her blue eyes and the fullness of her lips as her mouth formed a moue, as though she was disappointed in his decision to go alone. Any reply she would have made was interrupted when his mother coughed lightly and stared at Miranda. Some unspoken communication was shared in that moment by the two women, and he watched as Miranda sat up straighter, if that were possible, and closed her mouth, her lips now forming a tight line.

A memory flashed through his mind and he saw Miranda at their first meeting. The only daughter of one of their neighbors, a wealthy landowner with a minor title, she had been invited to a country dance at his family's estate. Drawn by her vivacious personality and her welcoming smile, he had asked her to dance. He could still see her dark blond curls, hanging down to her shoulders, shimmering and gleaming in the candlelight as they'd danced. She'd been generous in gifting him with her smiles, and they had laughed through the steps of the dance, then gone in to supper together.

Her standing, with the sizable portion she would bring to him in their marriage settlement, was deemed high enough for his status as the second son of a duke, and their marriage was accomplished the next year, even before his brother and the heir of the family married. Shrugging off the past that could not be changed, Adrian realized that he was staring at her.

Uncomfortable with what haunted him from his past and what faced him in the near future, Adrian nodded at his mother first and then his wife. "I fear I have much to accomplish before I can be on my way." Retreating into good manners, he bowed to them and walked to the door, which was opened for him by a footman. "Good day to you both," he said as he left, feeling for the first time a certain trepidation at leaving Miranda in the clutches of the dowager.

Chapter Three

Once Adrian left, there was nothing else to say. The dowager would choke before admitting to a curiosity about her son's motives or activities. Their weekly encounter was at an end, and Miranda tried not to let her anticipation at being released from the dowager's presence show. She placed the half-empty cup of tea back on the table in front of her and stood. Tempted to demonstrate her precedence over the dowager, Miranda instead decided that respect for her elders should win over her internal desire for the deference that should be afforded her due to her title.

Until Miranda produced an heir, or even a daughter, the dowager would see her as the still-less-than-acceptable wife of a second son. No power on earth could change her regard, or lack of it. Lowering her head in a courteous bow of sorts, Miranda walked to the door of the drawing room and hesitated only a moment as Cordelia's ever-efficient butler pulled it open.

Every week, after such a visit, Miranda found herself fighting the urge to tear her bonnet from her head and run screaming down the street like a madwoman bound for Bedlam. Years of practice won out and she stepped across the walk and climbed into the waiting carriage. As she took her seat and Fisk entered and sat opposite her, only a slight tremor in her clasped hands belied the blank expression she knew she could affect when needed.

And it was needed now.

"When you walk and sit as though you were wearing cast-iron stays, it tells me you have visited the dowager."

Miranda tried not to laugh, but the irreverent attitude of her friend ruined her efforts. Letting out an uncommon giggle, she smiled and removed the bonnet from her head.

"My stays are of the regular sort, I assure you, Sophie," she said, still smiling as she sat down on the paisley-covered chair. "Though I do confess to never allowing myself to relax when in the presence of Her Grace."

Her schoolroom friend held out her second cup of tea this morning, but this one Miranda looked forward to enjoying in informal company. Only a viscountess, Sophie was not considered by the dowager to be an appropriate companion for the Duchess of Windmere. But their friendship had been forged in the trials and challenges of the Hayton Academy for Young Ladies. The teachers there, as well as the owners, were as formidable as Her Grace, Cordelia, Duchess of Windmere and, without knowing it, they had prepared Miranda well for the constant struggle of living up to such lofty expectations.

However, where Sophie's marriage had become one of joy and the felicity of a good bond, Miranda's had not quite lived up to her girlish hopes and dreams. The Viscountess Allendale's life was filled by an attentive husband, two lovely sons, a London house and their country estates. The emptiness of her own was glaring by comparison. Something must have shown through, for Sophie reached out now and patted her hand.

"A rough visit, then?" Sophie offered a smile. "It could be a blessing somehow that Her Grace is dependable for something. If you are looking to ruin someone's happy mood, you certainly know where to send them."

Sophie's green eyes softened with concern. Pushing her loosely-gathered brown hair behind one shoulder, Sophie shook her head at Miranda, undermining her own belief in the words of rationalization she offered.

"I cannot imagine what has me so blue-deviled today," Miranda replied. Sipping the tea, she waited for her nerves to settle. "Her Grace was no different than any other time."

"Will she return to the country soon? I do not remember her staying in town this long before."

She shook her head. "I fear not. Juliet was presented and is having her first season. Her Grace will persevere until she has secured a suitable offer for her cherished goddaughter."

Surprised at the bitterness that entered her voice, she continued, "But Windmere is returning to the country."

"Windmere? Leaving while Lords is sitting? I did not think he shirked his duty." Sophie looked at her and tilted her head. The narrowing of her gaze was never a good sign for Miranda. "Something else is wrong here. I can feel it."

"As I said, I am simply out of sorts this morning."

Miranda smoothed her hair and leaned farther back into the seat cushions. Sophie on the scent of something new and intriguing was more persistent than Lord Bernard's champion hounds. Miranda should have gone directly back home after the encounter with her husband. One look at the intensity on her friend's face told her that it was too late for evasive maneuvers.

"What happened with Windmere?" Sophie's voice was soft with concern.

"He got drunk and missed dinner...." Miranda stopped herself before revealing the more private appointment he'd missed.

"Men always drink. I've seen Windmere drink a fair amount before. That is really not surprising."

Miranda looked at her friend. "He was completely foxed. Carrying on in his chambers, using vulgar language and throwing things. Even his valet tried to shield me from it. I do not remember him ever in this condition."

Frowning, she thought back to the words he'd yelled, but his efficient servant's coughing had covered most of them. She smoothed her skirts over her legs before looking back at Sophie. Skipping over the more personal details, she went on. "Then this morning he unexpectedly announced that he was leaving for Windmere Park and would be gone for some days."

Sophie stood and walked over to her chair. Pulling a small stool alongside, she sat down on it and took her hand.

"Did he harm you, Miranda? You may tell me not to inquire, but did he hurt you during his attentions?"

"Sophie! How can you ask such a question?" Miranda tugged her hand free and moved back from the viscountess. "Windmere would never raise a hand to me."

"I wasn't speaking of his hands, Miranda. If he were drunk when he visited you for…conjugal intimacies, he could have done much harm. Are you well?"

She could feel the heat of embarrassment enter her cheeks. They had never spoken this candidly about such a topic, and Miranda was not certain how Sophie even knew.

"Come, Miranda. I know what your life is like since your husband became Duke of Windmere," Sophie whispered more softly. "You both take the responsibilities and duties to the limit of serious, and your days, as set out by the dowager's designs, are ruled by conformity and regularity. You once let it slip that he visited your bed on Thursdays, so it is not so unusual to expect it would be every Thursday."

"He did not visit last evening."

"Did he visit *her?*"

"The dowager?" Sophie's eyes narrowed and she shook her head. Miranda then realized of whom she spoke: Windmere's mistress. "Of that, I have no idea."

"Have you told him that you care?" Sophie asked.

"I do not know what you mean. I care not that he has a mistress.'Tis the way of things."

"John does not have one."

Miranda glanced at Sophie and met her direct gaze. The dowager had made it quite clear that men of Windmere's rank were expected to have a woman available to satisfy their baser needs. And that it was no concern of Miranda's. Although their marriage had started out differently, Adrian's move to the title had changed many, many things, including the physical side of their marriage.

"It is unseemly for a wife to…" Miranda began, quoting one of the dowager's favorite admonitions.

"It is unseemly for a wife to ignore these signs of which you speak and act as though nothing is wrong. Miranda…" Sophie took her hand once more "…I would not encourage you to investigate this unless I was convinced that you are interested in your husband's well-being and that of your marriage. You were so filled with life and anticipation when you first married. You had such a *joie de vivre,* and I thought that Windmere returned your feelings."

"That was so long ago, Sophie, and so much has changed between us," she said with resignation.

Any hopes she'd had had been eroded by each new responsibility and new duty of being a duchess married to an important peer of the realm. So many depended on him that she'd learned to stand back and become what he needed the most: a wife who understood her place. Now, they were both so changed from the man and woman who'd stood before the rector at Windmere House and exchanged marriage vows. And she was not certain that either of them could go back to the people they had been, even if they wanted to.

"If that were true, you would not be in the least bit perturbed by anything he did or said or *did not do.*"

Sighing, Miranda stood and walked toward the door of the drawing room. If nothing else, she was curious. Surely it was only that? Gathering up her bonnet from where she had tossed it, she placed it back on her head, securing the ribbons beneath her chin, and tugged on her gloves.

"I will return home and see if he has left yet."

"A fair beginning. Call upon me if you need any assistance. Anything," Sophie called out to her as the door was opened.

Sophie had done enough already, Miranda suspected. As her carriage moved through the streets of Mayfair toward home, she began to silently practice the words she would use to inquire as to any difficulties the duke might be facing. It had been so long since she'd permitted herself to ask personal questions of him that she feared even knowing how to phrase them.

And what if the problem involved Windmere's mistress? Should Miranda simply turn away and let it be?

How could she overcome the embarrassment and humiliation of having brought up such a personal concern?

News from the butler, however, gave her all the time in the world. Adrian had left word that he was out for the remainder of the day, would return very late this evening—no need to wait for him—and that he and his valet would leave for Windmere Park at dawn. She could send word of any problems to him there, through his secretary.

How exactly did one ask one's husband through an intermediary the types of questions she was considering? Miranda spent most of that and the next few days pondering her next move and then decided that, in the proper way of things, a wife did not ask. But she also decided that she would. If there was any chance, no matter how slight, of peeling back the layers and reclaiming the man she'd married, it was worth the risks.

Three days after the duke left London for their estates in the north of England, the duchess received a note from her friend that caused her to send her own polite regrets to Lady Crispin and to the dowager. It would appear that neither the Duke nor Duchess of Windmere would be present for the ball on Saturday next, after all.

Chapter Four

Adrian watched out the window of his study as work on the estate continued as usual. His breathing had eased now, but he'd suffered two attacks during his travel here. Usually, the air felt easier to breathe in the country than in London, where the ash and dust and fog could make it rather uncomfortable. So long as he stayed away from the stables and the gardens, he remained free of those attacks the physicians and apothecaries called "hay fever." It was the others, the more virulent, breath-stealing ones, that seemed to be on the increase.

The last seven days had been grueling for him—first traveling north to Windmere Park and then the extensive review of all his estate and family documents. If his steward here thought it strange that he should appear and demand to see all the records, he would never say so. They'd ridden to outlying farms, visited the rector in the village that lay on his property, and spoken to many of his tenants. Repairs and some changes to the summer and autumn crops were planned where needed. A larger selection of books was ordered for use by the rector's wife to teach the children of the village.

The most difficult task yet lay ahead of him. His solicitor should be arriving either this day or the next, and Adrian would review and update his will. Although his title and most of the accompanying estates were entailed, he still had some discretionary properties and funds. He would feel better once those decisions and arrangements were made for everyone who depended on him for support or a living.

Turning from the window, Adrian picked up the glass of wine and drank from it. He'd learned the hard lesson of overimbibing the night he'd discovered his fate. His stomach had remained unsettled for days, and he'd had to stop several times on the road north to empty it rather forcefully. No, he would rather face his future, limited though it might be, with a clear head and a calm stomach.

It would be a few hours until supper even with the earlier country hours, so Adrian decided to walk down to the lake. He mentioned his intent to the butler as he picked up his hat and made his way through the house. Using a side door in the blue drawing room, Adrian followed the path that led away from the house to the larger of the two lakes in Windmere Park.

The sun beat strongly and its heat could be felt, in spite of the cool breezes that moved through the trees surrounding the lake. Seeking refuge from the strongest of its rays, he found a well-spread chestnut and sat down next to it, leaning against its stout trunk. The irony of facing his own impending death, even as every living thing was moving toward bloom and maturity, was not lost on him.

As was his custom, he reviewed the list of unaccomplished tasks left to him on this trip and realized that in his haste to leave the city, he'd not had the latest concoctions made up. The crumpled papers were most likely still in the pocket of his coat, where he'd shoved them the next morning. There was an apothecary of some experience whom he usually frequented some miles away in Newcastle, but also a woman in his own village who had gained some measure of good repute as a healer. Perhaps he would visit her.

Adding it to his mental list, he moved on to the next item. The estate and his personal papers were in order. Everything would be ready for his…demise. Adrian pulled off his hat and, tilting his head back, closed his eyes.

How did one approach this? Never an overly spiritual or religious man, he did not feel compelled to seek out a religious advisor. He trusted that the rector would perform the necessary rites with the solemnity Adrian deserved. When his symptoms worsened and he was convinced the end was nearing, he would speak to the rector about it. But not now.

The matters of the entailed estate were handled, those

of his own properties and will would be, and the only ones left were…his family. His mother and his wife.

His mother and his wife.

Shaking his head, he knew there would be no way of avoiding those subjects once his solicitor arrived. Although the estate documents included arrangements for both of them, he would verify the specifics and clarify what each woman could expect for an income and home after his death.

What would become of each of them? The strange thought formed in his mind and he knew that it was the thing that bothered him the most.

His distant, twice-removed cousin Robert would inherit the lands and titles and, since he already had the prerequisite heir-and-a-spare, the dukedom would go on. A pang of regret pierced Adrian then and he tried to discover its cause.

Never meant to inherit, he had come almost reluctantly to the titles and the powers and the responsibilities of being Duke of Windmere. And the primary responsibility after taking control was to produce an heir. In that, he and Miranda had failed. Perhaps that was the source of his discontent? No son of his own to inherit? Not even a daughter to convey everything entailed to a son of her own?

Racking his brains would make no difference in this. He picked up his hat and stood, dusting off his clothes as he did. Tugging the hat into place, Adrian began the walk back to the house. He suspected that once his solicitor arrived and everything was in order, his mind would cease struggling with the questions and ramifications of his death, and he could seek out ways to spend the time he had left.

Dinner and the rest of the evening were spent in quiet reflection as he examined his life. When sleep would not come, he walked the halls of Windmere House. He visited rooms he'd not seen since his childhood and was surprised to find that some of his toys were still stored in the nursery, waiting for small hands to find them. From the window of the bedchamber where he'd spent his visits home from the university, he spied the tree that had been the site of many adventures for him and his brother.

Dawn found him as restless as the night before, so he called for a horse and rode over the lands that had been his for such a short time. Only when the sun reached high in the midday sky and the loud protestations of his stomach could no longer be ignored, did he return to the house for rest and food.

The butler woke him to inform him that a coach had arrived from London. No instructions need be given about the hospitality required for guests at Windmere Park, so Adrian sent word that he would see Anderson at dinner. Spending time in the country had its advantages, the foremost in Adrian's mind being that of earlier and less formal meals. His household knew his clear preferences, and that, coupled with the fact that most of his neighbors were in London, assured him of uninterrupted time with his solicitor.

Now, drinking a glass of claret in the drawing room, he awaited the man's arrival. A clamoring outside the door drew his attention and he turned as the footman opened it, admitting not his solicitor, but his best friend.

"Parker! What are you doing here?" Adrian stood and strode over to his unexpected guest.

"Your cryptic note about your sudden departure did more to inflame my curiosity than to appease it, so I am here." Parker accepted a glass of claret from the butler. "Is it nearly time to eat? We did not stop for a noon meal."

Adrian looked to the corridor but saw no one else. Had Parker traveled with the solicitor then?

"As soon as Anderson arrives, we will go in to dinner. I'll have them set a place for you."

"Anderson?" Parker shook his head. "The man sent word that he is delayed in London and will not arrive until tomorrow. Surely we need not wait that long?"

At Parker's dry wit, Adrian shook his head. "I received no such word."

"I am, I fear, the messenger in this, Windmere. I ran into him at your house in London and have now delivered the message to you." Parker held out his glass and watched as it was filled again. "Where the devil is she?" Walking to the door, he peered out.

"She?" Alarmed, Adrian turned to the door. "Who

did you bring here?" Surely not. Surely, Parker would not have brought….

"Here now! If your thirst is not overwhelming, we can go right in," his friend was saying.

"Good evening, Windmere. My apologies for holding you up from your meal."

Miranda.

She stood in the doorway, with an anxious frown on her brow as though waiting for his anger. Relieved that Parker had not brought Caro as he'd suspected, Adrian walked to greet his wife.

"I did not expect you, madam," he said, lifting her hand and touching his lips to it. "I said there was no need to accompany me here."

He felt her shiver at the sharpness in his voice. He needed time alone to deal with his fate and did not want the complications that a wife presented. However, he could ascertain her reasons over dinner and send her back to the city on the morrow. Before he could say more, Parker pushed Adrian aside and offered Miranda his arm.

"He said the same thing to me, Your Grace, and you can see how much weight I gave his words. Come, the butler has assured me that dinner is ready."

After a glance at him and a moment's hesitation, his wife laid her hand on his friend's arm and off they walked down the hall, following the butler to the private dining room. Indeed, his staff knew of the changes to his plans, for three places were set at the oval table, all to one end, as he'd requested for the two originally planned. He watched as Parker escorted Miranda to one of the side chairs and then took a place opposite her. Adrian then sat in the chair at the end, with his wife on his right and his friend on the left.

At his nod, the butler and his assistant began serving the meal. Parker shoveled food into his mouth at an alarming rate. Without stopping for more than a breath or a swallow of his wine, he devoured two bowls of cream of lobster soup along with a small loaf of bread. When there was a slight delay in serving the next course, he continued to tear a slice of bread into pieces and push them in his mouth.

"Are you certain you only missed *one* meal?" Adrian asked. Parker did not even have the decency to look embarrassed at his behavior.

"Traveling the long roads here over these last… How many days did it take us, madam? Four?" Parker mumbled the rest as he finished chewing.

"It did take four days, although we arrived a bit earlier today than I had thought possible," Miranda replied softly.

Irritated by their friendly manner and the very fact that they were here, Adrian snapped out what he'd wanted to ask from the first moment.

"Why are you here, Miranda? I told you that this trip was simply to handle some family business. There is no entertainment here. No parties or luncheons to attend. No balls to dance at. I would think that the amusements of the city would have held your attention longer."

The room grew silent and even the servants paused in their actions at his tone. It was only the briefest of pauses, but he marked it. Parker choked as he chewed, and then swallowed loudly and washed his food down with another mouthful of wine. When he cleared his throat, Adrian got the message. For Miranda's part, the only reaction to his rude words was a slight fluttering of her eyelashes and her refusal to meet his gaze.

Any response was interrupted by the arrival of the next course. Plates of roast venison and leg of lamb were placed on the table, as well as boiled turnips and sauces for all the dishes. Adrian took up the carving knife and cut slices of the meats for each of them. At Parker's glare, he added a few to his plate. It was as he cut into his own food that Miranda answered his question.

"I have felt a bit overwhelmed by the demands of the Season, Windmere. I thought a short respite to the country might do me well."

"Overwhelmed by the dowager's demands, more likely," Parker interrupted. Pointing at her with his fork, he continued, "And now that she is sponsoring that chit in her first season, I would guess she's dragging you from one end of town to the other."

"That chit? What do you know of my mother's social activities?" Adrian felt the odd man out in this discussion.

"She cornered me ever so politely at Lord Hanson's soiree and made it clear that as your friend and close associate, I had a duty to help bring out the chit—excuse me, Miss Stevenson."

"And your reply?" Adrian asked. It wasn't often that someone got the better of Parker. Of course, his mother was, candidly, quite formidable when she desired to be so. And she'd made no secret of her desire for a successful launching of her goddaughter into polite society.

Parker blinked several times and frowned at him. "What do you think I told Her Grace? I agreed, of course."

Not to be deterred from his original question, Adrian turned back to Miranda. "Are you well?"

A hint of a blush tinged her cheeks and the corners of her mouth rose in a slight smile as though she was intrigued at some private thought. Then she met his gaze and shook her head. "I am well, Windmere. It is just that your mention of the country reminded me that, at times, I find it so much less tiring than the tedium and closeness of town."

Adrian winced at the formality of her address. He sensed that the one expressed was not her only answer. But, in company, even just Parker, he decided he would not press her for more. To articulate more concern than necessary would make her presence into an issue. And it would make it seem more important than the inconvenience it was. It was a simple case of not having the solitude he'd anticipated when he'd journeyed north.

He turned back to his food and silence filled the room, interrupted by Parker's occasional chomping noises. How had the man made his way in polite company? A few minutes later, filled from the hearty and flavorful food, Adrian pushed back and suggested that they proceed to the billiard room. Although Parker looked as though he would argue, he swallowed the mouthful of food he had just forked in and nodded.

Chapter Five

Miranda had looked away as she finished her words, not wanting to allow her lack of candor to show. Luckily, her husband seemed to give up on his chase for ulterior motives at her appearance here. At least, he had for now. Finished with her food, she dabbed at her mouth and laid the napkin on the table. She rose as the footman held her chair, and walked behind Adrian to the masculine sanctuary he favored so much when here at Windmere House. She wondered if he knew that billiards was a favorite of hers and that she played frequently…when he was not present.

She took a seat near the fireplace and watched as her husband and his friend chose their weapons from the rack of billiard sticks. They exchanged typical boasts about the upcoming game and even placed bets on the outcome. Tea arrived and she sipped hers as the even match went on.

"Would you be completely offended if we removed our jackets, madam?" Parker asked some minutes later. "I know it's terribly informal, but…" His words drifted off and he smiled that infectious smile of his as his hair fell into his eyes once more. He tossed his head to shake it back into place.

"I am certain that my constitution and sensibilities can withstand such an informality, sir. Only as long as we are in the country, of course."

"I told you she would be game, Windmere. Now nothing, not even too tight a fit, will stop me from defeating you," Parker boasted, as he shrugged his jacket off and tossed it on a nearby chair.

As she watched, her husband removed his, too, but instead of carelessly throwing his, he folded it and laid it over the back of a chair. Without their jackets, it was an easy thing to compare them. Both men were tall, with Parker having several inches over her husband. Both were muscular, but Adrian's build was a leaner one than his friend's. She could well understand that after seeing how much food Parker ate in a given day! In coloring they were opposites, with Adrian being the dark-haired one and Parker the blond Adonis.

After spending four days on the road with him, Miranda decided Parker definitely reminded her of the Adrian she'd known early in their marriage. An irreverent sense of humor pervaded his personality and behavior, but at the heart of it was a man of honor and caring. Drinking the now slightly warm tea, she wondered when Adrian had changed. She placed her cup back on the side table as she thought about it.

Not in the year they'd spent engaged to be married and not in the first year of their marriage, either. He was still the same outgoing man even during the terrible time of his brother's death and their year of mourning. It was after they'd put away the colors of official grief that something changed deep within him.

Instead of resisting the dowager's every command and directive, Adrian accepted them. Instead of plotting his own course for the dukedom he'd inherited, he followed the one left by his father and brother before him. Instead of the affectionate relationship he and Miranda had had, he began to distance himself from her, insisting that his mother's ideas of the proper way to do things were what he wanted for them.

Pulling herself back from her woolgathering, Miranda watched as the match drew closer. Startled as he laughed out loud at some whispered threat from Parker, and pushed him away to the other side of the table, she enjoyed the moment of camaraderie between the two of them. Not accustomed to seeing him so, she wondered why he hid it from her.

Why did he not let down his guard with her as he did with his friend? Was she the only one from whom he'd withdrawn this side of himself? Did he share this with his mistress?

Laughing.

Spontaneous.

Playful.

Caring.

Attractive.

Miranda's stomach roiled as the uncontrolled thoughts forced themselves forward. This kind of introspection did no good and now she felt truly sick as images of her husband and his paramour flashed fleetingly through her mind. She knew what the woman looked like—someone who disdained Miranda for her humble origins and had wanted to embarrass her had pointed out Mrs. Robinson in the park one day. She'd passed the woman by without any acknowledgment, of course, but she'd seen her clearly.

"Call for her maid, if you please." Her husband's voice broke into her reverie. Blinking to clear the now-gathering tears from her eyes, she saw that their game had stopped and they were both watching her.

"You see, Parker. It is as I suspected. The duchess is not well." Adrian approached and crouched down before her. "Her complexion is now turning green."

Parker rang for the footman, who was sent off for Fisk. Then he walked closer, squinting as he leaned down to her. "Was it the soup, do you think? Something spoiled at dinner?"

Miranda took a deep breath and shook her head. "I think that I am simply overtired from traveling. If you will excuse me," she said as she stood, or tried to, for her legs would not hold her up. Pausing for a moment and allowing Adrian to offer her his arm in support, she took in another deep breath and felt her head clear a bit. "I will seek my chambers and recover more thoroughly from the journey."

Parker backed away and allowed Adrian to escort her to the door. Fisk arrived and Miranda was released into the maid's efficient and meticulous care. She turned to take her leave and noticed Adrian's quiet scrutiny. He did not ask anything else of her, but wished her a good night's rest and nodded as she turned away.

It was as she drifted off to sleep that she realized it was Thursday evening.

Day was full upon them when Miranda next opened her eyes. Even the drawn curtains at each window could not disguise how high the sun was in the sky. Guessing it to be early afternoon, she pushed the covers aside and slid from the bed. As her feet touched the carpet, the door to the hallway opened and Fisk entered.

"What time is it?"

"Half past one, Your Grace. The duke gave orders that no one should disturb your rest," she said as she held out a dressing gown for Miranda to slip into. "The house does not have its full complement of staff, so it was easier than most times to insure that you would not be disturbed."

"Is the duke busy?" Miranda tied the gown and sat at her dressing table, allowing Fisk access to her hair for arranging. "Something simple, if you please."

"His Grace has been closed up in his study with his solicitor since early this morning, Your Grace. Other than a call for some food and wine to be served to them there, no one has seen or heard him."

Their lives did not intersect much at any time, least of all in the country, so Miranda decided to invite the rector and his wife to dinner. Tempted to include her husband, she hesitated, for his opposition to her presence was quite clear. She would stay out of his way for a day or two and then see if she could approach him with her questions.

"If the weather is as fine as it looks from my window, I plan on taking advantage of it and sitting out in the gazebo. Would you have Cook send some chocolate and a roll out to me there?"

"Of course, Your Grace. Should I join you there?"

Fisk stood and helped her out of her night rail and into a yellow day dress that had short sleeves and was trimmed in white ruffles. After taking the proffered matching bonnet, Miranda shook her head. "There is no need. You may remain inside."

Miranda picked out a book she'd been intending to read and walked through the house, out a side door, and found the gazebo surrounded by pleasant sunshine. Once her chocolate and roll arrived, she sat quietly and read the book she'd chosen.

Actually, she tried to read, but irritating and bothersome thoughts kept creeping into her mind. Finally, she put the book down on the table and considered her options.

She'd learned over the last four days of travel that there were many things about her husband that she did not know. Lord Parker had regaled her during their time in the carriage with tales of his and Adrian's visits to the various Windmere estates and other places in England. Even a hunting lodge in Scotland that Miranda did not know the Warfield family owned. When he'd looked embarrassed about having mentioned it, she knew it was used for the type of event a wife was not invited to attend.

She'd learned last night that her husband could be stubborn and secretive. Something was indeed going on, and he did not want her interference. His words clearly told her she was an inconvenient interruption to his plans.

The wind blew a loose curl free and it fell into her face. Miranda tugged off the bonnet and laid it on her lap, rearranging the curl.

She'd also learned, by her own weakness and reaction to the thought of his more personal relationship, that she would not be able to broach such a subject with him. They'd adjusted over the past few years to a certain level of marital involvement, and, although it was not the warm and personable one she'd dreamed of having with her husband, it was clearly his choice.

She smiled at her own folly. A momentary lapse in the duke's behavior did not mean he wanted things to change. It meant that he was simply a man. She should have waited for something more significant than one night's overindulgence to signal a change in him…or a crack in his ducal veneer.

"You do make such a lovely sight, Your Grace."

The words and Lord Parker's approach startled her out of her thoughts. "My lord, you surprised me." Shading her eyes to see him in the bright sunlight, she realized she had no bonnet on.

"Pardon for barging in on you here, Your Grace. I've been bumping around the house and grounds and not having much success finding anyone else. Well, at least anyone who is not engaged in some earth-shatteringly important endeavor that cannot be interrupted."

He looked confused and then laughed. "Not that your activity here is not as important—that is, not as…"

Miranda held up her hand to stop him. "I took no offense at your words," she said, pointing to an empty chair. "Join me if you care to."

As they slipped into a pleasant conversation about the estate, Miranda realized that she'd spoken more to Parker in these last few days than she'd spoken to Adrian in years.

He tugged the curtain aside once more to watch her. From his study he had a clear view of the gazebo on the western veranda and its occupants. His wife had been alone for some time before Parker had joined her. They seemed to rub along quite companionably. Parker had told him of the journey north from town. Although she still looked pale, Miranda did appear recovered from whatever had ailed her last evening.

"So, that is the extent of the settlement for the duchess? No property, no title?" Adrian turned to face his solicitor.

The terms of the will and the entailment were not a complete surprise to him—without a male heir to inherit directly, everything moved to his grandfather's other line. His mother had also inherited an income from her eldest brother, so her future was quite settled.

Miranda was a different sort of problem. With her widow's jointure, she would live closer to the edge of genteel poverty than to the standards to which she'd become accustomed. When they had married, her dowry had replenished his family's depleted coffers and allowed him, on his accession, to make much needed improvements on the grounds here, as well as on the other family estates. Her father, overwhelmed by the prestige of joining his with the exalted Warfield family and Windmere name, was not overly concerned with carving out a protected settlement for Miranda. And he'd been willing to pay for the privilege of his daughter marrying even the second son of the esteemed Duke of Windmere.

Within a few years, changes unthought of and certainly unanticipated had occurred, and the second son held the title. And after his death, she would have a small allowance and be granted a place to live on the grounds of Windmere Park. As the widow of the previous duke, with no family to take her in, she would be an outsider.

Still an outsider.

As she'd always been.

Turning back to the window, he watched her talk

quite animatedly about something with Parker. Then she stopped and her smile disappeared. Instead, she stared pensively out toward the lake and nodded her head at whatever question she'd been asked.

It was only a thought at first. Then it tickled Adrian's conscience and drew his attention. He watched as some sadness overtook her, and he found himself opening the window. For what, he knew not. Drawing away, he tried to discover the source of his discomfort.

"Your Grace? Should I continue?"

"Let us break for a bit. I should like to walk to clear my head," he said, nodding at the man.

Anderson agreed readily and gathered his papers into neat little piles before standing and bowing to him. Adrian waited for him to leave his study before opening the door that led out to the gardens. Striding quickly, he approached the gazebo and listened to the conversation.

"Rubbish!"

"I assure you, Parker, though it may sound as though I boast, I could do it."

"An affront! That's what it is. An affront to my honor," Parker replied with the theatrics of a man intensely insulted.

Adrian's curiosity got the better of him and he asked the obvious, drawing their attention at once as he approached. "What could you do, madam?"

He stared at her and she placed her bonnet back on her head and then stood to greet him. He had enjoyed the sight of the wind catching little tendrils of her hair and pulling them free of the arrangement that her maid had done up. Part of him wanted to tear the hat off and run his hands through her hair, loosening it until it fell below her waist. His body took no more than a moment to respond to the feelings engendered, with a clear message of intent. Blinking, he shook off the odd thoughts and turned his attention back to his wife's boast.

"Your duchess claims that she could best me in a game of billiards. Is that not audacious?" Parker said, offering a bow to Miranda. "Couldn't be true, could it, Windmere?" His friend looked horrified as he contemplated the very thought of it.

"Is it true, Miranda? I have not seen you play in many a year." Adrian realized it was before their marriage and before his mother began her campaign to make Miranda a suitable wife for a man bearing the Warfield name.

"I did not mean it as a challenge, sir," she began. He watched her eyes light with a mischief he had not seen recently, and she nodded to Parker. "But it is a fair statement of my abilities."

Adrian walked to where she sat. "It would seem the only *fair* thing to do is to offer Parker the chance to defend his honor. Rather than an appointment at dawn, would you be willing to settle for billiards after dinner?"

"Actually, I have an engagement for dinner this evening. Could we play later?" Miranda looked at Parker for an answer.

"Are you having guests or going somewhere?" So

used to having separate schedules and social engagements, Adrian had no idea of hers.

"The rector and his wife are coming here, Windmere. You are welcome, of course." She had not hesitated, so he felt the invitation was genuine. He also had not known that she was on social terms with Reverend Grayson and his wife. "I did not ask because I did not want to interfere any more than I have with your business here."

He almost answered with a quick excuse, but she turned her gaze on Parker then and he was not certain he wanted his friend there without him being present, too.

"And you, as well, Parker. You might enjoy meeting the Graysons."

Parker turned a bit pale and shook his head. "I appreciate the invitation, of course, but meeting with a parson is not my idea of entertainment." He shot Adrian a look that implored *Help me out of this situation,* and Adrian laughed.

"I would enjoy that. Shall we plan on holding the challenge at, say, nine this evening?"

Miranda smiled and looked from him to Parker and back. "Nine it is, then." She stood and so did Parker. "I will not keep you any longer, Windmere." With a nod, she picked up the book on the table and walked back to the house.

She had just closed the door when the coughing erupted. Deep spasms racked Adrian's chest and, as he turned away from the gazebo, he groped in his jacket and waistcoat to find the small bottle of syrup that usually quieted them. Tugging off the small cap, he leaned his head back and poured some of the thick, brown concoction into his mouth, then swallowed. Lowering his head, he looked into the face of his friend. In his haste, Adrian had forgotten all about Parker.

A few more coughs escaped before he felt his chest loosen and calm. Searching for words to make light of his symptoms, Adrian opened and closed his mouth. To his surprise, it was Parker who spoke first—in a tone much too serious for a lighthearted rogue of his nature.

"Your cough has worsened?"

"It is just the flowers. Hay fever, the physicians are calling it," Adrian said, trying to brush aside any concerns.

"No, Adrian. It has worsened. I have noticed it lately. You have more of these spells and I have witnessed you drink from that bottle more times now than even a few months ago."

Startled at the familiarity, Adrian shook his head and tried to deny the assertion. "It is just this time of year."

Parker walked closer and spoke in a quiet voice. "I know there is more to this than you willingly will admit. Just know that I am here for you if you need anything."

His gut tightened as he realized the importance of this. Parker had noticed the changes. Who else had?

"Do not add disclosure to your list of concerns. We are in each other's pockets. I could not help but notice. Others who see you occasionally have not."

Adrian turned back and looked at the path that Miranda had taken.

"The duchess is another matter altogether," Parker added.

"What do you mean?" Had he given himself away that night when he'd been drunk and rambling? Although Thompson assured him nothing had been heard by the servants or the duchess, he was not so certain.

"I had an opportunity to get to know her more during our travels here. I think she senses something is wrong and does not know what to do about it." Parker stepped away. "*Is* something wrong?"

Not ready or willing to part with the secret yet, he simply changed the subject. "Anderson is waiting inside for me. Will I see you at dinner?"

The dismissal was effective. They both took a polite step back and nodded. Turning away, Adrian felt some measure of guilt clawing at him. After too many years spent distancing himself from friends and family, as was befitting someone in his station of life, his mother would say, he now did not know how to bridge those distances.

He returned to his study and remained there, closed up with Anderson, reviewing the remaining papers and documents so important to his demise and what would follow. When his solicitor excused himself with plans for a walk and then a dinner tray in his room, Adrian went and prepared for dinner. Anticipation within him grew as he thought about the evening that lay ahead.

Chapter Six

Miranda was a bit different in recent days and something about that difference made the evening to come one he more eagerly anticipated. He dressed more casually than he would have in town, and walked down to the drawing room at the time Thompson told him the duchess expected the rector's arrival.

Adrian walked in and obviously interrupted a conversation in progress. They stood and greeted him formally and then took their seats again. From the tone and subject of the talk, it was clear that the rector, his wife and the duchess were well acquainted. Adrian accepted a glass of claret from the butler and stood off to one side, ready to observe before participating. Parker's arrival surprised them all.

"Lord Parker! You did come." Miranda stood and approached his friend. "Let me make you known to the Graysons. Reverend Grayson and Mrs. Grayson, this is Baron William Parker. Lord Parker, the Gray-sons."

The Graysons greeted Parker, who looked as though he'd been forced to attend, and everyone took a seat. Adrian still stood and sipped from his wine. A footman entered and whispered something to Miranda, making her smile. She stood, as they all did then, and announced that dinner was ready. Parker offered his arm to Miranda and she placed her hand on his sleeve. Adrian did the same with Mrs. Grayson, leaving the rector without a lady to escort, and they all walked into the hall.

Once they were seated and the first course served, conversation flowed as freely as the wine and ale did. Adrian learned more about Miranda during that meal than he had in years. She served on many of Mrs. Grayson's committees and endeavors to help the people of the village. She spent most of her time while here in the country on those tasks. She preferred to be here rather than in London. Not only did she play billiards, but she favored several card games as well as fishing in the lakes and streams of Windmere Park.

With Miranda seated next to him rather than across, he took an opportunity when Parker and the rector were discussing something of interest to both of them, and leaned over to speak quietly to her.

"I cannot imagine that my mother knows about your proclivity for fishing and billiards."

Miranda paled a bit at his words. "I do not believe

that she does. I try to keep certain facets of my life out of her view."

"Still critical, then?" he asked.

"Always."

Miranda began to turn back to her food when he asked another question. "Then why do you visit her each week? Surely you do not enjoy being in her company?" He knew of no one, from his long deceased father to the now highly touted Miss Stevenson, who could tolerate his mother's overwhelming ways.

"It is one of the duties I carry out as Duchess of Windmere. She has invited me for a weekly appointment and I attend. Like so many other obligations, not one of my choosing, but mine nonetheless."

In other words, no matter how unpleasant or odious the duty, she would strive to hold up her end of the bargain. He had never thought about what she had been going through these last years as he'd been learning and taking over the reins of one of the largest and now most profitable estates in England. With each passing week and month, she'd seemed more self-assured and busy, so he'd never pursued any explanation. His mother had confirmed that Miranda was applying herself to the tasks facing her.

He leaned back in his chair and continued eating, although he would never be able to identify any of the foods he put in his mouth. He could only suspect that this change within him was brought about by the knowledge of his impending death. If he had not been forced to examine his conscience and his life, he would never have comprehended how Miranda's own life was so different for her.

She would have gone on, fulfilling her duties, attending to the call of his mother, living a separate life, and he would have been completely unaware.

And now? Now that changes to their lives, to their marriage even, would matter not? Was it fair to her to let her go on believing that she would continue as duchess?

"Now it is Windmere's turn to look ill."

Parker's voice broke into Adrian's reverie. "Me? Do I look ill?" He tried to shake off the discomfort his friend's perusal had caused. "I am well."

"The duchess did the same thing last evening. Turned pea-green and looked like she would topple into her soup bowl." Parker then grimaced at the words he'd chosen and nodded to Miranda. "Beg your pardon, madam, but you did."

"I assure you all that I am well, and I thank you for your concern. Now, if everyone is finished, shall we move to the drawing room for dessert and coffee? Or tea if the ladies wish?" Adrian stood. "I suspect that Parker will need something more fortifying to prepare him for his challenge."

The rector laughed. "I do not approve, as a whole, of games of chance, but having seen the duchess's abilities firsthand, I shall look on this as a defense of honor."

Parker appeared irritated now.

The Graysons, claiming the lateness of the hour and

the journey back to their home, took their leave before
the announced match, so Adrian found himself once
more to the side, watching his wife. She moved gracefully around the billiard table, sighting and lining up her
shots and leaning over to shoot. He found himself
watching the arch of her neck, the curve of her hips and
the way she blew out of her pursed lips to move the single curl that seemed to land in her eyes no matter how
many times she tucked it away.

Soon, she held him in thrall. His body reacted as
though he'd not had a woman in months. His groin
tightened and he shifted his position to ease it. Her
throaty laughter and light but not inappropriate jesting
with Parker were added enticements. Adrian had not
thought to feel this kind of passion for her again, not
when their relations had become routine and he had
found another woman who kindled fires within him.

Now, his wife had him burning to bury himself in
her warm, willing body and seek some satisfaction—
or solace?—within her. If he had not thought himself
changed by the revelations of the last week, he knew
it now.

Bringing his attention back to the game, he watched
as Parker struggled to keep his lead after several skillful shots by Miranda. She was about to win. Parker was
no longer taking the game and the win for granted, and
his face became red as he tried harder to stay ahead of
her. The last shot was hers and both men waited to see
her take the win in this challenge. Adrian had no doubt

that Parker, the aplomb necessary to win now dwindling, would be a gracious loser. He hoped.

Miranda took her place and bent over to get closer to the ball. With a slight hesitation, she drew back her stick and then sent it skidding on the felt, barely touching the ball, which spun several times but did not move any closer to the target. Her turn over, Parker jumped into position, made his shot and shouted loudly as the ball dropped into the net under the corner pocket of the table.

"By Jove! That was a wonderful game, Duchess. I had no idea that you would be such a piece of competition." Parker strode over to her side, lifted her hand to his mouth and kissed it. "My compliments on a game well played!"

Adrian could no longer hold in his mirth. Parker either had no idea of how close he'd come to disaster or was ignoring it. Laughing loudly, Adrian walked to her side, lifting her now-released hand to his own mouth. "My compliments as well, Miranda." He kissed it and then added, "For allowing my deluded friend to believe he won!"

Miranda, he could see, fought a smile and stuttered out some words, but Parker growled in indignation. "Allowing? Allowing me to win? I do not believe it!"

"My lord, the win was obvious to all of us. Skillful play, as you said."

Adrian noticed that she never said it was Parker who'd played skillfully. A nice evasion and just the thing to save a man's self-esteem. She smiled then and the heat rose in him. He wanted to kiss her, to taste her mouth and to touch his lips to hers, not something they did often.

"Parker, if you will excuse us? Her Grace mentioned that she would like to retire immediately after your game."

He waited for her to deny his words, but she did not. Instead she nodded at Parker and handed her stick to the footman to return to the rack on the wall. Then, as Adrian held out his arm, she took it and walked by his side from the room. Not certain of the reason for his actions, he said not a word as they proceeded up the stairs and down the corridor that led to their chambers.

So many things ran through his mind, but his body knew only one—he wanted her. If she felt the growing tension, she did not reveal the fact. She walked at his side, matching her step to his, until they reached her door. He turned to face her, wondering what her reaction would be to him visiting her bed on other than a Thursday evening.

"My thanks for not embarrassing him too badly, Miranda," he said, smiling. "Parker's mistake was in underestimating you."

"Was that a compliment, Windmere?" she asked, tilting her head to meet his gaze. Searching his face, her eyes narrowed as she continued. "Or do you feel duped, as well?"

"I do feel hoodwinked, now that you speak of it. I had no idea of your conquests here," he said, stepping closer to her. "I had no idea of your abilities in other than social situations." He lifted his hand to touch her cheek. Her eyes closed for a moment as though savoring his caress, and then she stared at him with a sort of terrified fascination. "I had no idea of the enticing woman you'd become while I was looking away."

He slid his hand around her neck and brought her closer. He hesitated for a moment, waiting for any sign that his attentions were unwelcome, and then claimed the lips and mouth of a woman he'd known and yet not known for years. Her mouth softened beneath his, much as her body did when he joined with her, and she leaned into him as he tasted and kissed her, over and over.

Adrian took another step, bringing him in close contact and placing her between the closed chamber door and his body. Now he held her face with both his hands and covered her lips with his. He felt her hands creep up to his arms, not in deterrence, but in encouragement. A noise from inside the room startled them both into realizing where they stood, and he released her slowly from his grasp, taking several more kisses from her caress-swollen lips.

"Your pardon, Miranda. I..." he began, but could come up with no words of true apology. He wanted her, he wanted her now, and the fact that they were standing in the hall within sight of anyone, any servant or guest who chose to walk there, be damned! He cleared his throat and started again. "I would join you in your chambers. If you have no objections?"

Would she refuse him? He would never force himself or his attentions on her, but prayed in the next several seconds that she would not rebuff his request.

"If you would give me a few minutes to prepare, I will be ready for your…" Now it was her turn to trip over her words, and he lightened inside. She looked away and then back at him. As he watched, the tip of her tongue slid out and moistened her lips as though they had gone dry. A pulsation of desire racked his body and he found that his breathing was becoming too quick.

"I shall visit you in a quarter hour, if that is acceptable?" How he forced the words out, he would never know.

She nodded and then reached for the doorknob. He did not move as she stepped backward into her room, closing the door in a swift but quiet movement. He wrestled with the passion that flowed through him and leaned against the wall next to her door, waiting to regain some measure of control before moving away.

A quarter hour was not too long a wait.

Miranda closed the door and rested her head on it, not daring to turn toward her waiting maid. She knew her cheeks were flushed and that her lips were swollen from Adrian's attentions. But the worst, the absolute worst, was that her breasts were also swollen and her nipples tight and hard, and she could feel the friction of them rubbing against her shift, above the stays that held her breasts in place.

Unwilling to expose such a condition and even more

unwilling to think about what it meant, she took a slow, deep breath and waited for her body to calm.

It did no such thing.

Instead it rebelled. The reactions to his kisses flowed through her, bringing heat and desire to all kinds of places in her body. And she decided that her sensitive breasts were not the worst, after all.

That place between her thighs, where Adrian would join their bodies, now throbbed with heat and moisture in anticipation. Even though she tried to remain detached from her feelings, Miranda knew she could not.

"Your Grace? Are you well?" Fisk's voice was filled with concern. "Is there something amiss?"

Nothing that His Grace between her legs would not solve.

Miranda stood back from the door, turned and nodded. "I need to wash up. His Grace will be here shortly."

Although she tried to sound matter-of-fact, she knew she'd failed when Fisk let out a surprised gasp. But her practiced maid recovered much more quickly than she did.

"Here now, Your Grace," Fisk said as she began to pour some water into a basin, which she placed on the table near the fireplace. "Let me help you with your dress first."

In a few efficient minutes, Miranda was undressed, washed and dressed in a soft linen night rail and silk dressing gown. In spite of her objections, Fisk unpinned her hair, and it fell in loose waves over her shoulders. Then her maid opened the door to her bedchamber, and Miranda found herself standing before her bed with a candle in her hand.

Walking to the side table, she placed the candlestick there and lifted the covers to climb in. Some small sound alerted her to Adrian's presence and she saw him standing next to the door that connected their chambers.

He wore a dressing gown, but she could see no trousers and or shirt beneath it. Her body reacted to the sight of the curly hair on his chest, which she knew would rub against her breasts as he thrust inside of her. Crossing her arms over her own chest to try to rid herself of such sensations, she waited for his approach.

"Miranda," he said in a whisper. "Miranda."

She shivered at the passion in his voice and he smiled a wicked smile. It took but a moment for him to stride across the room and pull her to him, taking her mouth as he had in the hall. This time, however, there was no interrupting servant or lack of privacy to limit his ardor. Her thoughts scattered and she could only feel him and his touch on her. Somehow her dressing gown and night rail were gone, as was his, and the heat and hardness of his body pressed her down onto the bedcovers.

As his hands moved over her, she felt as though she was being caressed by a storm—quick-moving, tumultuous and overwhelming at times. Then he knelt between her legs and spread her thighs, all the time staring at her with a heat that made her body answer his call. His touch there soothed and inflamed as he slid his fingers into that place and found the spot that he knew would drive her further into arousal.

And it did. Everything within her tightened with every stroke. He moved his legs apart now and lifted her hips to his hardness. Unable to look away from his passion or his body, Miranda felt herself pulse and shudder as he leaned forward and thrust inside her. She gasped as he filled her and began to move, each stroke bringing her closer and closer to the edge.

Then he took her breast in his mouth and suckled on it with as much ardor as he had kissed her lips, and she felt everything in her dissolve. She clutched at the bedcovers as he pushed against her, over and over again. He moved his mouth to hers as she let out the keening moan that built inside her. Her body arched against his as wave after wave of pleasure enveloped her. Adrian matched every throbbing wave with another thrust until she felt him harden and thicken and then his release was upon him. Leaning his head back, he groaned loudly, not trying to mask the sound of his pleasure.

Their breathing labored, they lay as they were, both spent from their shared passions, until Adrian lifted himself from her a few minutes later. Miranda found that in spite of her unusual position—atop the bedcovers with her legs hanging over the side of the bed, exposing her to his sight—she did not have the strength to move.

He picked up their clothing and tugged his dressing gown into place, tying the belt at his waist. Then he reached out to assist her to rise. With gentle care, he guided her back into the night rail and placed the dressing gown over her shoulders. Miranda could say nothing as he lifted the bedcovers and helped her into her bed.

Stunned by what had happened between them, she watched silently as he kissed her on the forehead and stared at her with a haunted expression. Then he walked away.

Not certain of what to say, she waited until he'd left and then turned away from the door, burrowing farther under the covers so he would not hear her. All manner of inappropriate thoughts and feelings threatened her as she gave in to tears. The most improper was, of course, her desire to repeat the passion between them.

Not until that moment did she understand how much she had missed him since they began living separate lives. Not until then did she regret the distance in such a profound way. Not until that time did she acknowledge even to herself that she wanted her husband back.

As they had been when they married.

Husband and wife, with no mother or mistress between them.

And Miranda was willing to do whatever was necessary to get him back. Forever. Well, she thought as she sniffled, for their natural lives, at least.

Fortified with resolve, Miranda wiped her eyes and felt the pull of sleep upon her. Tomorrow would be a good time to begin her campaign.

Chapter Seven

After a night spent tossing and turning, alone in his bed, Adrian decided he owed Miranda an apology. His actions last night toward her had been unforgivable.

A gentleman did not behave that way to a lady. He'd plundered her body for his own satisfaction, never once considering what she wanted or did not want.

Of course, the sight of her standing in the shadows, outlined by the flames of the fireplace and the flickering light of the candle she carried, was partly to blame for his lack of control. The layers of her gowns, rather than covering her, had exposed her curves to him clearly. And the erect nipples she'd tried to cover with her arms aroused him more than any words could have.

But when she'd leaned down to lift the bedcovers and her dressing gown gaped, displaying the sloping curves of her lovely breasts, he could not stop himself. Within minutes, he'd found himself buried to the hilt in her softness. He had to blame the noises she made, the moisture that wept from her private places and the way her body answered his every touch, for propelling him to pillage her as he never had before.

Running his hand through his hair, he shook his head. Clearly, that was no way to treat a lady. Especially when that lady was your wife.

Looking at the wooden pier that jutted out into the tranquil lake, he searched for her. Her maid and the butler reported she'd gone for an early morning walk and not yet returned. In the misty light, it was difficult to see far, but he did spy a boy from the village sitting on the pier with a fishing pole in his hand. Perchance he'd seen the duchess? Adrian walked down to the water's edge and called out to him.

"Boy? You there!" he called out, his voice echoing through the stillness. "Have you seen the duchess?"

The boy gave a start and pulled his hat lower on his brow, but did not turn or speak to him. Adrian strode to the pier and stepped onto it, approaching from the side. Once more, the lad turned so that his face was hidden.

Irritated at being ignored, Adrian called out again, much louder than need be. "Boy! Do not ignore me!"

The youth shuddered with each bellowed word and Adrian finally reached his side. Tapping him on the shoulder, he spoke. "Do you know who I am, boy? You should not ignore the Duke of Windmere, upon whose pier you fish and upon whose condescension your family relies."

The boy put the pole down, tucking it into a knot in one of the planks to secure it, and turned to face him. Lifting his hat from his head, he released, to Adrian's surprise, masses of long, curling hair that fell down his back.

Him?

Her! Miranda's blue eyes glittered in amusement now as her deception was revealed.

"Windmere," she said simply.

He glanced at her attire and found that she was indeed dressed as a boy, in knee-length trousers, a rough shirt, waistcoat and jacket. Stockings lay rolled in a ball and tucked into shoes at her side. Although the clothes were those of a servant, the duchess appeared quite comfortable in them. Even the scandalous trousers.

"What is this, Miranda? What are you doing dressed like this?"

"A morning dress or even riding habit simply do not work while fishing, so I wear these. I never thought you'd see them." He held out his hand to help her to her feet. Her bare feet.

"My mother cannot know of these," he said, pointing to the garments she wore. "Apoplexy the extent of which I cannot begin to fathom would follow if she discovered you dressed like this."

But as he looked at the way the trousers fit over the flare of her hips and exposed her lower legs and shapely ankles to his inspection, Adrian could think of several reasons why he liked these clothes on her. And how it would be to take them off of her, one piece at a time until her soft flesh was the only thing in his sight.

Egad! Had facing death turned him into a randy goat? With each glimpse of her, he wanted nothing so much as to take her to bed and not let her go.

He'd felt last night as though he was searching for something when he filled her. His release had brought him closer to his goal, but not the deeper sense of what it was he needed. How did one look for something when one did not know what it was?

"No, Windmere. I am careful when I dress like this and where I store these clothes for my use. And who sees me thusly."

Devil a bit! Others had seen her this way? Feeling something that felt like possessiveness, he shook his head. "I do not think your appearing anywhere like this…" his gaze moved over her and his body reacted strongly—again "…is a good idea. Who knows of it?"

"Please, Windmere. If you are angry over this, please do not seek out those few who simply followed my orders. This is my fault, if anyone's," she implored. Reaching out, she touched his arm. "I promise never to repeat this inexcusable breach of behavior."

He searched for the words to say to her. Was he angry? No, of all the reactions pulsing through him, anger was not one of them. "Without me," he whispered harshly.

"Excuse me, Windmere. What did you say?" She leaned closer to him and cocked her ear to hear him better.

"Without me, madam. The only time I want you in these garments is when I am present."

"I do not understand. I only wear these to go fishing here on the estate."

He stepped close and gathered the lapels of her jacket in his hands. "And you have reeled in your last catch of the morning, Miranda. Although I am certain this is not what you meant."

She did not struggle against his hold or his kiss. As a matter of fact, she stood in his grasp as she had last night, a willing participant. However, she probably thought he had only a kiss in mind, when indeed he had so much more planned.

He moved his lips over hers until she opened her mouth and let his tongue in. Tasting and teasing, he touched her tongue with his until she followed his lead. He broke away from her and looked over her head at the shoreline. More of this and they would both plummet off the pier into the water below.

Adrian took her hand and pulled her to the edge of the lake. He leaned her up against the trunk of a weeping willow tree and began to unbutton the waistcoat and shirt she wore. It was strangely exciting to see that she wore a sheer linen shift underneath the coarse outer garments. Before he touched her, though, he stopped and looked at her to see if she objected to such handling.

"Tell me no and I will stop."

She searched his face for a moment and then smiled at him. His resolve not to manhandle her dissolved before that smile, and he leaned down and gave her the last soft kiss he would remember. Then she leaned her head back against the tree and closed her eyes, giving him the leave he needed to pursue the satisfaction he wanted for both of them.

He spread the now-unbuttoned edges of her shirt and touched her breasts, lifting and feeling their weight and teasing the tightened nipples with his thumbs. She sighed and he continued. Bracing his knee between her legs, he slid his hand toward the waistline of her trousers. Could she be naked underneath these?

His hand met soft linen once more and Adrian loosened the buttons and flap and reached inside. She wore those feminine undergarments that covered each leg and tied at the waist. Sliding his hand deeper into the trousers, he found the opening and touched her thighs and then the place between them.

It did not take long for her trousers to be thrown aside and his opened. Then, against a tree by the lake, the duke let fly his amorous attentions and he took the duchess again…and again. When he could collect his thoughts, he knew he owed her several more apologies.

He was pacing at a furious rate in front of the fireplace in the blue drawing room when she arrived. Her body still hummed and a few places still throbbed from the waves of satisfaction that he'd produced with his attentions by the lake, so she found it difficult to rush back through the stables. He'd agreed not to follow her, giving his word as a peer of the realm, so she went back her usual way, reclaiming her clothes and dressing in the small tack room.

When she'd escaped the house this morning, Miranda believed that an hour or two fishing would calm her nerves from the evening before. She had no idea that the sight of her dressed in servant's clothes would have such an effect on the duke. Surely his reaction was proof of the scandalous nature of a woman in men's garb, which she'd been warned of so many times.

Now, with the pale blue morning dress back in place and her hair gathered behind her head, she entered the room.

"Windmere? You called for me?"

He came to an abrupt stop at the sound of her voice and turned to face her. Still dressed in the clothes he'd worn when they had…they had *met,* he ran a hand through his hair, pushing it from his eyes. When their gazes locked, she could see many things revealed there, but it was the guilt that confused her.

"Please, be seated, Miranda." Adrian nodded at the footman, who brought in a tray of tea and then left, closing the door firmly behind himself. When they were alone, her husband spoke again. "I find that I owe you an apology for my recent behavior."

Puzzled by his words, she poured the tea and waited for it to cool. He took a sip from his cup—coffee, she thought, and very strong from the smell of it. "An apology, Windmere? I cannot think of what you've done to owe me such a thing."

Actually, with the dowager's words ringing furiously inside her at this very moment, she could think of many transgressions of the bounds of acceptable behavior committed by both of them, but more by her than him.

Following her husband to the country against his express orders to the contrary.

Traveling in the company of a single man, even with an ever-present maid.

Behaving in an informal manner simply because of their location far from town.

Treating the gentry as though they were equal to peers of the realm.

Allowing men to discard their clothing in her presence.

Not maintaining the prestige and elevated position of the Duchess of Windmere and the Warfield family name.

Conducting marital congress outside the bedchamber, in the light of day, in sight of anyone who chose to walk by—while dressed in a manservant's clothing.

Shaking her head, she discounted the latter, for she was sure that her state of dress or undress would matter not to the dowager. The former was the much more grievous lapse in behavior, she was sure, for persons of impeccable breeding would never have considered the first and gotten to the second…or third parts of the sin.

"In spite of any permission you may have granted, my attentions to you were abominable, Miranda. A husband does not attack his wife simply because his passions get away from him."

Abominable? No, she thought not.

Overwhelming. Breathtaking. Scandalous. Habit-forming. But not abominable. She sipped her tea before replying, because all sorts of additional inappropriate thoughts were flying through her mind.

At the heart of it, she remembered her vow to herself that she would do whatever it took to get her husband back. If that meant somewhat tumultuous physical activities, she was not opposed to them. Actually, with the way her body felt at this moment, all warm and relaxed, she was even *willing* to engage in such behavior.

Then she realized what he'd said. Could she ask him? Bah! She needed to be bold to win the day, so she did.

"Your passions got away from you, Windmere? Truly?" She felt guilty about hunting down a compliment, but she asked, anyway. Convinced that things between them were different now, she felt confident about his answer.

"I confess to that, Miranda. One moment I felt in complete control and then the next, well, you know what happened next. I cannot explain it, but I can only apologize for such forceful…attentions."

Miranda decided that she needed to know, once and for all, the cause for the change in her husband. It went deeper than simply behaving differently; it went to something inside him.

"Is this need of yours for more forceful attentions,

as you call them, related to your recent dismissal of your mistress?"

Sophie's note had included specific details of their parting, including the number and cost of the gifts given to the woman to ease his way out her door. "Information or ammunition," Sophie had written. Miranda decided that, if things were going to be different between Adrian and her, now was the time to use it, and she watched and waited for his answer.

Her husband turned red and coughed several times. Not the choking kind that he suffered from time to time, which seemed to come from the base of his lungs and threaten his consciousness; no, these were more surprised-by-her-words coughs. He finished by clearing his throat and taking a mouthful of his coffee.

"How do you know of that? Of her?" he asked quietly.

Both of them knew this was outside the bounds of what they should ever be discussing. If Miranda were smart, and she did not think herself a beetle-headed ninnyhammer, she would rise from her chair and bid her husband good day, leaving him and the insulting topic behind. If she were not now infatuated with the possibilities between her and Adrian, she would accept his apology and return to the normal behavior between them. If she were not ever optimistic in spite of years of learning the folly of it, she would never press him for this admission.

"I did not think it was a secret. I know of her in the customary ways."

Servants' gossip.

Ladies' gossip.

Gossip.

Miranda knew when he'd begun seeing Mrs. Robinson and even where and when he spent time with her. She knew where the woman's house was—one rented with the duke's funds, she was assured—and which jeweler he favored for purchases to meet "Caro's" fancy tastes. Thinking of it now, while also remembering the personal things he'd done to and with Miranda herself this last day, made it hurt in a way it had not hurt before.

"So is this change in behavior simply the result of not being able to relieve your baser needs on your paramour, then? Will your wife suit your purposes until you find another fancy piece to take Caro's place?"

Horrified that she'd spoken such words, Miranda blinked and looked away. The silence stretched on until she glanced back at him. He opened and closed his mouth several times, as though changing his mind at his answers. She was certain that this was the first time he'd been asked such a personal question.

He must have remembered himself in the next few moments, for he straightened up and his face lost the glow and ease of the last few days. The Duke of Windmere now glared at his audacious duchess.

"Exactly that, my dear." He put his cup down on the table and walked back to the fireplace. Leaning his arm on the mantel, he continued without ever meeting her eyes. "A short aberration that will not happen again. I plan on rectifying the situation upon my return to town." He did look at her now, with those polite eyes of the past five years. "I leave for London tomorrow. Please let Thompson know if you will be traveling with us. Or possibly you'd prefer to go at another time?"

She felt as though he'd slapped her squarely across her face, and she flinched at his cold tone now. Her skin felt clammy and her stomach heaved at his rebuke. Pulling herself back, she retreated to the practiced civility that he had.

"As Your Grace wishes, of course." Clearly, he did not want to suffer her company back to town.

"Well, then. I still have business to see to before I leave. You will excuse me?"

It wasn't truly a question, so he did not wait for her response. With a nod, he walked from the room and the footman closed the door behind him. Even the loud rough coughing that erupted from the duke in the corridor did not give her any measure of satisfaction.

Miranda sat unmoving on the chair, clasping her hands tightly in her lap. This was the reason one did not behave inappropriately—the pain in her heart crushed her and threatened to crush her soul, as well. Regardless of any change to him these last few days, Adrian Warfield was still the Duke of Windmere with all that that entailed. And she was the Duchess of Windmere.

And damn her foolish heart for forgetting that for even a moment.

Chapter Eight

"Why did we push off now?" Parker asked, taking a seat opposite him in the coach. "And where is the duchess?"

"The duchess prefers to travel back to town by herself." Adrian did not know if that were the truth or not, but he would not admit it to Parker and bring about another round of griping and whining.

"That's not so, Windmere. Her Grace told me on our way here that she dreads the journey to and fro Windmere Park."

Probably not as much as she would dread being trapped in the same coach with him now. Her blue eyes, wounded and filling with tears, haunted him. His cruelty had been deliberate, but even he was surprised by the depth of the damage it did to her.

Adrian used his walking stick to bang on the roof of the coach. They were off a moment later, first to the village and then to London. The attack that struck him as he'd left the drawing room had been the worst in months. He'd spent the rest of the day and night in his room, trying all the various remedies that his physicians had prescribed—the medicaments, the inhalants, the syrups and concoctions.

Now, worn out from it all, he wanted to settle back in the cushions and sleep. First, though, he needed to stop to see the woman in the village who had a reputation as a healer of sorts. He'd long ignored the stories of her success, relying on the more professional advice of physicians. However, a death sentence opened him to other options he would not have considered in the past. He would have summoned her to the estate, but this would keep the gossip to a minimum.

"So what did you do that made her retreat to her rooms? If you were angry over the game, you should have told me so."

"I was not angry over the billiards. If anyone should be angry, it should be you. She beat you by letting you win."

"I won that game."

"Keep telling yourself that. I think if you will examine how it went, you will understand how she drew you in, waited to pounce and then *let* you win."

Adrian leaned his head back against the bolster and closed his eyes. This trip was going to be a long and tiring one if Parker continued harassing him each mile of the way.

"Perhaps you are correct, Windmere."

Adrian opened his eyes and gazed at his friend. "Why the sudden change?"

"Other fish to fry." Parker met his gaze with a level one of his own, but Adrian sensed more in those words than a simple reply. Fish to fry? Fish? Fishing? Bloody hell!

They'd been seen. Parker's satisfied expression confirmed it.

Before he could question him, the carriage rolled into the village and stopped in front of the building that served as public rooms and an inn. Adrian would walk the short distance to the cottage of Mrs. Gresham. He'd sent word ahead so she would be there.

She pulled the door open as soon as he reached it, and Adrian found he needed to stoop over to enter. Once inside, he greeted her.

"Your Grace," she answered with a curtsy. "This is my granddaughter, Annabelle. She helps me with my gardens and my herbs." The girl appeared to be about ten and six, and she curtsied, as well. "If you have no objections, Your Grace, I would like her to hear your symptoms, since she aids me in my work. Her discretion can be trusted."

He nodded and took the seat offered to him. Mrs. Gresham began asking him questions and, before he realized it, nigh on an hour had passed. Adrian could tell that she did not favor the practice of bleeding a patient, nor cupping. She frowned, shook her head and tsked when he mentioned how many times those procedures had been applied to him. The two women consulted together and looked over the newest prescriptions from the physicians before making their recommendations to him.

"This first one is fine, Your Grace, but I would suggest ignoring the other two," Mrs. Gresham began as she handed the doctor's note back to him. "Instead, try these as a tea—boil the water and steep three crushed leaves for each cup. Two to three times a day. The trick of this is to prevent the lung spasms from occurring and causing further damage."

Her granddaughter handed him several paper-wrapped packages as the older woman explained each one. "This one—add this to a good brandy or a licorice liquor and sip it when the worst of the spasms are upon you. No more than three-fingers deep in one of your fancy snifters at one time. Have your man make a small amount of it ahead for when you need it.

"This one should help your sleep," she added.

"Laudanum?" He held up the small dark glass bottle and peered into it.

"No, Your Grace. Laudanum is something to be used with extreme care and only occasionally. This is the extract of an herb I have found helpful in inducing a healthy, deep sleep."

He listened carefully to the instructions, including those about his daily schedule, his diet and exercise, and the avoidance of certain substances and animals. Mrs. Gresham gave well-formed opinions and reasons for each recommendation she made. She suggested leaving the city before the worst of the summer heat was upon it, making the air not only soot-filled but overheated, as well. And she agreed with the doctors' suggestion of taking the waters at Bath as a way to invigorate his breathing and to ease the tightness in his chest.

He waited to ask the most important question until the end. Adrian stood to leave when they finished giving him advice.

"The physicians made a rather dire prediction. Would you agree with it?"

"Dire, Your Grace?" Mrs. Gresham stood and walked with him to the door. "What was their pronouncement?"

"That the condition has significantly deteriorated and my death may be approaching." He tried to sound calm about it, but this was the first time he'd spoken of it to anyone. "In less than a year's time."

The woman reached out and patted his hand as she probably did to anyone in her family or her neighbors in need of comfort. Certainly it was a first for him. "Your Grace, they have been monitoring your condition for some years, so I would not discount their observations. There is always hope that your condition may change. These herbs and suggestions will, at the least, relieve some of the symptoms that cause you such difficulty."

He reached into his pocket and lifted out a small purse. It contained several pounds, not the same amount the doctors charged him, but close. If her advice worked, it was worth anything he had. "For your time and trouble, Mrs. Gresham."

"Oh, no, Your Grace, I could not accept your coins." She backed away as though the purse were on fire.

"Use it to replace the herbs you have given me, then." He placed it on the table near the door and walked out before she could stop him. "I will call on you when I am back at Windmere Park."

The women curtsied again as he took his leave. Walking back to his coach, he realized that Mrs. Gresham had an inordinate amount of medical knowledge. Each of her explanations made sense, was based on observation or practice and seemed reasonable. His steward had highly recommended her, as had his butler, and even the rector had added to the praise over her manner of treatment and abilities.

It certainly could not hurt Adrian to follow her course of treatment and see if his symptoms improved. With death as his other option, it did not seem so far-fetched at all.

Reaching the coach, he waited for the groom to retrieve Parker from the public room, and then climbed in for the long ride to London.

Parker kept his own counsel for more than an hour, offering suspicious glances but no words. Adrian, for his part, fell asleep after that and avoided any questions until they reached their stop for the night. They made their way to a private dining room that had been reserved for them, and shook off the dust of the road.

The food was hot, filling and plentiful, and served quickly. Once their port was served and the servants left, Adrian knew he could evade Parker no longer.

"So, you went walking early yesterday morning, I presume?"

"I never thought you as foolish as that. Right under your wife's nose? You take a peasant girl against a tree at the lake where your wife takes her walks! Really, Adrian, what if the duchess had come upon you at that moment?"

"It *was* the duchess," Adrian said quietly, amused that his friend was indignant over an affront to Miranda's dignity.

"What did you say? The duchess? Surely not! This girl had long hair and wore men's clothing." Parker took a mouthful of the port and swallowed it. "Surely not?"

"I thought you were going to take me to task over my choice of a time and place for such activities, but I never realized you thought I would be so indiscreet as to have someone else while Miranda is in residence."

"The duchess agreed to such a thing? Wearing those clothes? And the rest?" Parker appeared to be thinking now about the scene he'd witnessed, drank more and shook his head. "I never once thought it was her. She's such a stickler, always so prim and proper."

"Before you think the worst of her, let me explain. Apparently the duchess is able to evade my mother on occasion, dressed as a boy. Miranda, as you heard at dinner the other night, likes to fish. As she explained it to me, her gowns and even her riding habit are impediments, so she arranged for a set of clothing for her use. 'Tis nothing more than that."

Adrian found that he did not like the possibility of his friend thinking too hard on the subject of his wife's lovely curves exposed by such garments. "The rest is personal and I would rather we drop the subject."

Parker nodded quickly, also uncomfortable with the direction the conversation would take if not changed. Filling his own glass with more port, Adrian thought of the best way to broach the other topic with his friend. He'd decided on the road from Windmere Park that he needed to be able to discuss the situation with someone, and that someone should be Parker.

"The last two weeks have been difficult ones, to say the least. I was given some disturbing news and it has thrown my equilibrium off completely. Actually, it has caused me to behave in a manner distinctly opposite from my usual habits and practices."

Parker sat down now and faced him. "This news? Was this what forced you from London?"

"I was not forced from London, but yes, this news necessitated me coming to Windmere Park to make certain arrangements."

"And did it also cause you to break your arrangement with Caro? That is why you gave her her congé before you left?"

"Yes. I had to end it with her."

"And this news? I presume you are ready to share it

with me? I assure you, Windmere…Adrian, I can be trusted with this."

"The doctors do not expect me to live past year's end."

Just as when Adrian himself had heard the news, Parker sat speechless for several minutes. His next re-action was unexpected—he burst out laughing.

"Quite the Banbury tale, Windmere! I commend you on your ability to joke about something so serious." He held out his glass in a toast and then downed the remain-ing liquid.

Adrian shook his head. "I only wish it were a jest, Will. I am serious about this. Deadly serious, if I may be gauche?"

Parker lost all the color in his face and turned the same shade that Miranda had a few nights ago—pea-green. Then, without much warning, he ran into the water closet, and Adrian could hear the retching begin almost immediately. He knew the feeling—although he'd drunk far more before casting up his accounts. A few minutes later, the door opened and Parker came out.

"Year's end, is it, then?"

Adrian nodded and Parker dropped into the chair next to his.

"That is bloody preposterous! The physicians can do nothing?"

"Only lessen the symptoms."

"Tell me the whole of it and then we can judge it," he said quietly.

They talked late into the night as Adrian explained

the history of his condition, the physicians' approach and now this new course planned by Mrs. Gresham. With the truth shared, Adrian found that the rest of the trip went by much easier. Now that he'd confided in his friend, he found himself more at peace with what he knew and what would be happening.

As they pulled in front of the house in Mayfair, Parker grabbed his arm and leaned closer so his words could not be overheard.

"What will you do?" he asked.

"Do? I've told you of my plans."

"What about the duchess?"

"What about her?"

"Does she know? Is that why things were so strained between you at Windmere Park? Why you did certain things which will remain unnamed?"

They had not spoken of Miranda since Adrian had revealed the truth. And Adrian had forced the guilty feelings he had over his treatment of her from his mind. The wounded look in her eyes still tore at him and he did not know how to fix it, or even if he could repair the damage between them.

"As I said, Will, I lost my better judgment in several situations with Miranda and have caused a breach between us. I think I should let it lie for now and think on it more when she returns to London."

"Egads, Adrian! What will she say? What will she think?"

"At this point, she might be wishing me to the devil."

"Never say that! Miranda is good-hearted and would never wish ill upon you." Adrian could see that Will had placed himself as Miranda's champion.

"I do not want her to know, Will. Not now." He'd truly not thought past the present moment.

"Do not say that you mean to keep her unaware of such a dire situation? She should know." Parker climbed out of the coach when the groom opened the door. Leaning his head back in, he repeated his earlier words. "What about the duchess?"

Indeed, Adrian thought, completely unprepared to deal with that issue. What about Miranda?

He spent the next five days avoiding his mother's summonses and finishing up arrangements begun during his meetings with his solicitor. Anderson was impeccable in carrying out his wishes, and soon all the estate documents were done.

Adrian attended two sessions of Lords, but sat quietly rather than getting involved in the debate or the issues that had seemed so important just a month ago. At his mother's behest, he presented himself at two balls and danced with Miss Stevenson before making his escape to his club or back home. Parker accompanied him to many of the events, never speaking of his condition.

Miranda returned to London about six days after he did, and she returned as the Duchess of Windmere. Gone was the brightness he'd seen in her face in the country. Gone was the spontaneity that had taken hold of her during that visit, the woman who had challenged his friend to a game, the woman who had melted in his arms, the woman who had dared to wear trousers to go fishing. Instead, it was the dowager's protégée who returned to Mayfair, and damn him, it was his fault.

Chapter Nine

"Quite a crush tonight!"

Sophie sat next to her in an area off to one side of the dance floor. Accepting a glass of wine from one of the footmen, she took one for Miranda as well.

Miranda nodded and fanned herself again. Far too many people crammed into far too little space, and then expected to dance. She'd never understood the appeal of such a gathering.

"Is Windmere still here?" Sophie looked around, but from their seats, it was impossible to see anyone past those immediately surrounding them.

"I wouldn't know," she replied blandly. Actually, even saying his name was difficult. Seeing him, across the room or across the table, was an excruciating reminder of her lapse in control. And of how impossible it was to put the genie back in the bottle after its release.

"I will take you to task for this. Remember that you will not behave this way without an explanation to me," the viscountess said, with a smile so wide it must have been painful.

Sophie's tone was playful so as not to draw attention from anyone near them, but Miranda understood it was a threat. Since her return to town, she'd taken up her schedule as though she'd never gone. Lunches, dinners, balls, shopping excursions, riding in the park, and on and on. All the time hoping that exhaustion would give her a night's sleep without making her suffer from the memories of that night. All the time hoping that immersing herself in the life she had would erase her dreams of a life she could not have.

Not satisfied with waiting, Sophie stood and peered over the heads of those closest. "Your Grace, it would appear that the duke is still here. Our husbands approach together."

What was this about? Miranda stood as the men broke through the throng and advanced slowly toward them. Greeting both, she forced a smile to her face as they chatted about the ball and whom they'd seen or spoken with so far. The orchestra began tuning up for a waltz when the men asked their wives to dance.

Since she and Adrian had not danced yet this evening, it would be poor form to refuse, so Miranda was trapped. At least the earlier dance given to Lord Parker had been a quadrille, where, other than a joined hand and some polite conversation, little attention was expected. And if truth be told, Parker had made himself scarce as soon as the dance was completed, so there was no opportunity to speak at length to him. She suspected he was simply doing what was expected of him—dancing with the wife of his friend when present at these social gatherings.

But this—waltzing with her husband—was different.

He held out his hand and she placed hers on it, allowing him to lead her to the floor. Taking their positions, she slid her hand into his and permitted his other hand to rest at her waist. Trying to remain calm, she focused her attention on the other dancers around them.

Sophie looked far too smug, as though something was in the works. Miranda watched as Lord and Lady Allendale exchanged words and gestures of familiarity. Although too close an embrace in this dance was frowned upon, the threat did not stop them from sneaking a kiss before the music began. Her heart hurt just watching them.

"I see that the Allendales are up to their antics once more," Adrian whispered to her.

She said nothing in reply, but waited as the violins played the opening strains. Then she followed Adrian's lead around the dance floor.

"You have been busy since your return from the country."

"So many things to do, with the Season in full swing, Windmere. Surely you know all about that?"

He drew her closer as they swept around the room, part of the large swirling crowd, but she held herself almost rigid in his arms. He leaned his head closer and drew in a breath over her head. "A new fragrance, my dear?"

Why did he do this? He was the one who'd drawn the line between them and insured she would not cross it by his cruel remarks that day. In a few minutes she would be free of his attentions and she could seek the balcony outside to regain her composure. She shook her head. "Nothing new, Windmere."

"Will I see you at dinner tomorrow evening? I have not spoken to you since your return." His voice was soft, but it struck at her like a weapon.

"I fear not. I believe I am engaged for dinner at the Wilkinsons'."

Another turn around the floor and it would be over. She focused on the flickering candles surrounding the room and the way they glittered in the heat.

"The next evening, then?"

"If you have Webb speak with my secretary, I am certain they can find a mutually acceptable date, Windmere." Almost there, the strains of the music reached the crescendo and started to wind down.

"I will speak to you later and we can come to an agreement," he said.

"Later, Windmere? Whatever do you mean?" He could not. He would not.

"I had planned to visit you this evening, my dear. If you have no objections?"

Miranda tripped over her feet and, if not for his grip on her hand and his strength, she would have taken them both down. As it was, she lost her footing and took several steps to regain it. She was shaking by the time she stopped. Looking at him in disbelief, she loosened his grasp on her hand and stepped away.

"I—I am suddenly feeling indisposed," she stuttered. "I fear tonight would not be a good night for…" she searched for a polite way of saying something that they should not even be discussing "…a *visit*."

The Allendales joined them then and the conversation changed topics. "Are you quite well, Your Grace? I saw you nearly take a nasty spill," Sophie exclaimed.

Grateful for the way out given to her by her friend, Miranda shook her head. "I think the strap of my slipper may have torn. Can you help me see to its repair?"

Within a minute, Sophie had snatched her from Adrian's grasp and they were heading not to the retiring room, but to the Allendale coach. Sophie also sent a note back to her husband informing him of the change, and letting him know that she would meet him back at home.

A while later, as the coach made its way through the streets of London, and they were sitting alone once more, Miranda knew she owed some explanation to her friend. But where to begin and what to say? Or did she even want to drag her misery out in front of someone so very happy with her husband and her life?

"What did he do to you, Miranda?"

"I simply tripped over my own feet and stumbled." She purposely ignored the true question.

A period of silence followed, broken only by the clatter of the horses and carriage moving over the stone streets.

"He informed me that he wished to visit my bed this evening and I refused." She sighed.

"I know that I am the cause of whatever has gone badly between the two of you and I am heartily sorry," Sophie said mournfully. "I seem to get carried away, thinking that everyone can be as happy as John and I are. He's chided me about getting involved and I think he must be correct in this."

"You cannot blame yourself for my errors in judgment, Sophie. I should have known better than to allow foolish dreams or hopes to cloud my responsibilities."

"And so that is the end of it? You walk through life as the Duchess of Windmere with nothing left over for yourself."

Tears filled Miranda's eyes and she nodded at her friend. "I will have so many things to do, I have so many things to do now, that there will be no time left over for anything but my duties."

She paused and looked out the carriage window as the city passed by. "I should be pleased that so much has been given to me, the daughter of a gentleman. I should be grateful that fate or God has seen fit to allow my husband to inherit such titles and lands and power. I should…not wish that his brother had never died."

"I know that you should not have any cause to do so, but would you listen to a suggestion I have to make?"

Sophie reached over and took Miranda's gloved hand in hers. Miranda nodded.

"The longer you stay away or keep him away, the worse it will be. If there is no other way, then treat his visit to your chambers as you do your visits to the dowager—a necessary thing you must tolerate." Sophie shuddered now, ruining the effect she was trying to make.

"In other words, return to how it was between us before this escapade of folly?"

"Can you, Miranda? I sense a certain brittleness in you now and it scares me. I worry that something will happen to you if you are not able to put this all back in the perspective you used to have of it."

Brittle? Yes, that's exactly how she felt. As though the wrong move or word or sound or person would happen and the facade she'd erected over her bruised heart would crack into a million pieces. Miranda was not certain if she could make the pain go away. But Sophie's face, filled with concern and guilt, made her nod.

"It is just what I will do, and actually have been doing, except, of course, for the duke's personal attentions."

The coach pulled up in front of Warfield Place and Sophie squeezed her hand again. The groom opened the door, flipped down the steps and helped Miranda out. The front door was already opening and so she left Sophie without another word.

Reaching her chambers, she had Fisk prepare her for bed, for Adrian would never be so impolite as to visit when she'd expressed her objection to it.

* * *

The woman, a wealthy widow who seemed to be on many of the best guest lists, pressed against his arm, allowing her well-endowed bosom to rub against him now for the third time. With the daringly low neckline of her dress, Adrian suspected he might be holding her breasts in his hands soon if she continued. He'd comprehended the real message long ago, but apparently was not responding as he should.

In spite of the mean words he'd spoken to Miranda on the issue, he had no intentions of engaging another mistress. Between facing his mortality and discovering the warm and willing woman that lived within his wife, he did not want another woman. He wanted her.

"Mrs. Dobbs, I see my friend Lord Parker coming. If you will excuse me, we have another engagement to make."

He stepped back but she followed. He waved to Parker to make him hurry. "Here now, Parker. I know I am holding us up," he said as he reached out to shake his hand and to force the avid Mrs. Dobbs away from him.

"Your Grace." Parker nodded. "Your carriage is waiting outside for you, as you requested."

"Ah, my thanks. Lord Parker, may I make you known to Mrs. Dobbs? Mrs. Dobbs, Lord Parker." The "lady" curtsied and then stretched out her hand to Parker.

"Charmed, ma'am," he said politely as he took it.

The necessary introduction accomplished, Adrian

turned to his friend and nodded. "Enjoy the rest of your evening, Mrs. Dobbs."

"Dorothea, Your Grace." She smiled and dipped into another curtsy that gave him another glimpse of her ill-disguised offering.

Unable to respond, Adrian backed away several paces, turned and walked toward the path that led around the house to the front entranceway, where his coach would be. He did not wait for Parker to follow, though he knew he would. As soon as they made it to the portico, his groom spotted him and brought the coach closer.

"To my club." He nodded to the driver as he climbed in. Parker sat down, the door was closed and they moved off, slowly at first, as his driver battled the crowds to get access to the street.

"Another friend of Caro's?" Parker asked, once the coach was moving.

"Yes, although 'friend' may be a bit kind."

Several of Caro's acquaintances had approached him to let him know of their availability now that he and Caro had parted ways. Word spread quickly when a man of his influence and wealth was looking, but in this case word was spreading even though he was not.

"I am not in the market for a new paramour, Parker."

"Then things are better between you and the duchess? I danced with her earlier and she seemed very distant in her addresses to me. Almost as though she was not there."

"I've made no headway concerning the duchess. As

a matter of fact, I have yet to get her alone to speak with her at all." Adrian smiled at his friend. "That will change tonight."

"And the rest of it? Will you tell her the truth? About what the physicians said?" Parker lowered his voice. "It doesn't seem right somehow to keep it from her."

"I do not want her to know. Not now. Not until I've made arrangements for her so that she'll have nothing to worry over."

"Worry over? She's the duchess. Isn't that enough?"

"Not without producing a child, it is not. An heir would enable her to live as she does now, even contribute her guidance to his upbringing. But without one, she is left with less than what she brought to our marriage."

"You would do that to her? I never thought it possible!"

"Not me, Will. The way the entail and letters of patent are written is unchangeable. But over the last few weeks, I have decided to set her up on her own so that she has no worries after I pass."

"What do you mean?" Parker looked at him with suspicion in his gaze. "Are you going to separate?"

"Actually, since producing an heir remains the priority of a man in my situation, separation is not an option," he began. Until he became incapacitated or cocked up his toes completely, begetting an heir was the most important thing he could do—both for the dukedom and now for Miranda. "If I can buy Caro a small mansion in a fashionable part of town, why can I not do the same for the duchess?"

"You don't plan on telling her this, either, do you?"

Adrian shook his head. "If the doctors are incorrect, then she would have worried needlessly. She's been a dutiful wife, Parker. Put up with the dowager. Always carried out her part of the marriage and even saved most of our property with the dowry she brought. The least I can do is make these arrangements."

Parker settled back in his seat and nodded. "So, do you think the physicians could be wrong? Do you need to see another? Was there some treatment they recommended that you did not do?"

"Any one of them could be wrong, certainly, but all three in consultation? I have been seeing Penworthy for a number of years. He suggested the others when my condition worsened and he could come up with nothing new or different. No, Parker, I fear that I've seen all the doctors I need to about this."

With a nod, Parker seemed to accept this news. Crossing his arms over his chest, he frowned again. "So what are your plans for the duchess? Where will you look for a house for her?"

"I thought over near the edge of Mayfair. A few properties have become available there. None so large that it would be unmanageable for her."

"I do not think the duchess will want to live there, Windmere. It is too much in the city. I think she'd prefer something out in the country. Near Allendale, perhaps?"

"I think I would know better than you what my wife would like, Parker. You overstep yourself in this."

"Did you pick out the house for Caro alone?"

Adrian grunted at the question. Parker knew that Caro had accompanied him to look at several places before choosing one. But that was his mistress. Personal involvement was part and parcel of the relationship. Miranda was his wife…

It did not make sense when thought of in that manner.

Instead of acquiescing now that he'd made his point, as any gentleman would, Parker challenged him again. "What is her favorite color?"

Adrian could not answer. He did not know.

"How old was she when she learned to fish?"

He shrugged. He did not know.

"What is the thing she did here in London that she says was the most fun she ever had?"

Damn him! How had Parker learned these things?

"Talk to her, Adrian."

"It was talking that got me into trouble with her," he grumbled.

That was not precisely how it had happened.

He'd been so overwhelmed by her knowledge of Caro that he'd acted in anger. He was not ready then to reveal the truth to her, so he'd struck out with his words. Then, realizing that he must be the one to make the first step, he nodded. "I will."

Parker rapped hard on the roof of the carriage. "To Warfield Place!" he called out loudly to the driver and groomsmen.

The carriage rounded a corner and headed in a different direction now. In a few minutes, Adrian would be home and he would begin his campaign to get to know his wife in order to set up a new life for her.

He climbed out when the groom opened the door, and stepped down onto the walk. "Take Lord Parker wherever he wants to go."

"Aye, Your Grace." The groom nodded as he closed the door.

"My thanks, Parker, for your insight into this," Adrian said as his friend looked out the window at him.

Adrian had turned to go in when Parker called out to him. "Red. Four. Skating during the Frost Fair."

The carriage rolled off and Adrian reached the door as he realized what Parker had meant.

Miranda's favorite color was red.

She'd learned to fish when she was four years of age.

Skating at the Frost Fair a few years before had been the most fun she'd had in London.

It was a start. For the first time since he'd learned of his fate, Adrian felt as though he had a purpose to fill these next months. First, of course, was to try to beget an heir, which would certainly make things inordinately better for everyone involved. The second was to make arrangements and get Miranda's new life set up in time.

He found himself in front of the duchess's doorway before he even knew where he was heading. Indisposed, she'd said at the ball. He thought not.

Chapter Ten

Miranda turned over and shoved her pillow aside. The night was dragging on and she despaired of ever having a restful sleep again. Every time she allowed herself to fall asleep, she would see him or hear him or, even worse, she would feel his hands on her in her dreams. Finally, she decided that a glass of brandy might help settle her nerves.

Pushing back the covers, she reached for the dressing gown and slipped it on. About to slide her feet into the slippers next to the bed, she changed her mind and pushed them aside. Rather than ring for brandy, Miranda chose to go to the duke's study where he kept his best stock. Maybe the walk would help her relax, as well. She could always pick out another book to read while she was near the library. Reaching the door, she opened it quietly and stepped into the corridor.

Adrian stood a few feet away, staring at her. She could think of nothing to say, so she looked at him.

"I hope I did not disturb you? I did not think I made any noise, but I must have if I awakened you."

"I was not asleep, Windmere." What should she do now? Back away into her room and close the door in his face? Stay and chat? She shook her head at that choice.

"Where are you going, then? Have you need of anything? Should I call someone to assist you?"

He seemed nervous, stringing question after question without giving her an opportunity to answer any of them. He was still dressed in his formal clothes from the ball this evening, but his hair was tousled as though he'd been out in the wind. His eyes glittered in the light of the candles in the sconce on the wall beside her door.

"I was going down to get a glass of brandy." She stopped herself from inviting him along, for she was not certain she really wanted him there.

"Really? I would love a brandy. May I join you? Or would you like to join me in my chambers for it?" He held his arm out to her and she had to accept. Then he shook his head and stepped away. "I suspect that I am the last person you would like to share a brandy with, Miranda, and I quite understand your hesitation." He stepped back and bowed to her. "If there is nothing else that you need, I will leave you."

He was like a storm again. She could see he was thinking of other things as he spoke, as though there were several things he wanted to say at once. She reached out and touched his sleeve. Maybe they both needed a drink?

"I would be pleased if you would join me for a brandy, Windmere." The words came out before she'd made up her mind to speak.

"Very well, then. Shall we go down to the study or my chambers?" he asked, nodding in each direction.

"The study would be my choice," she answered. "That was my original destination."

Now she placed her hand in his and walked by his side down the stairs. Although several servants approached to inquire if they needed assistance, Adrian waved them off. They entered the study and he lit several candles around the room. Miranda took a seat in one of the high-backed chairs and covered her legs with her dressing gown.

He went to the cabinet, opened it with his key and took out the decanter of brandy he kept there. As she watched, he took snifters down from the shelf next to the cabinet and filled them with the aromatic liquor. Without replacing the bottle, he brought one of the glasses to her and then sat in the chair behind the desk.

A few minutes passed as each sipped their brandy in the quiet of the night. Although she had nothing to speak of with him, she could feel that he was building to some type of conversation. Soon, he rose and looked out the window.

"I would speak quite candidly to you, Miranda, if you would allow it." His voice was soft and his words a request, not a command.

"Of course, Windmere." She sipped again, trying to fortify herself for whatever was coming her way.

"Your words to me about Caro…Mrs. Robinson… surprised me. I had never planned to insult you about what had happened between us that day and the night before. Indeed, I was quite overwhelmed by it."

Miranda felt heat creep up into her face and she rubbed at her cheeks. Whether it was caused by the brandy or his words, she knew not. She was only thankful that the light in the study was somewhat dim.

"You asked me if the change in my relationship with…her was the cause for h-how we…." He tripped over his words and then drank deeply from his glass, refilling it before he tried again.

He seemed to be having some difficulty coming up with words appropriate for a discussion between a man and his wife, and, as she knew, this was not really a topic they should be discussing.

"I just wanted you to know that what happened between us was not me seeking to satisfy my baser needs on you. I cannot explain the how or why of my trip to Windmere Park, but I found that your presence was an enticing distraction from my purpose there. And you seemed to show up when I least wanted or expected you."

"So, you did not want me there?"

"No, I did not. I said so to you when you asked about coming with me. But once you arrived, I found that I liked having you there. I saw you in ways I had not before and, well, the change was an arousing one."

Arousing? Even the very word conjured feelings within her. She shook her head. "You are confusing me,

Windmere. There seems to be something missing from your explanation."

He drank again before speaking. There was a long pause as though he could not figure out what to say, then he dragged another chair closer to hers, and sat in it. Fearing what she would hear, she took a mouthful of the brandy and let it slide down her throat and warm her stomach.

"Miranda, about three weeks ago I received some disturbing news. As a result of that news, I needed to handle certain business arrangements in a timely manner, and so I went off to Windmere Park to meet with my steward and my solicitor." He stopped and looked at her, gazing intently into her eyes.

"You told me not to accompany you. Were you planning on bringing Mrs. Robinson there?"

Did a man take his mistress to his ducal seat? Was that inappropriate or indecent? The dowager had not discussed that situation in the past and had issued no pronouncements on how the practice would be handled. However, Miranda suspected she knew the woman's opinion of such a scandalous event. And she knew the dowager's opinion of her even asking Windmere the question.

'Twas simply not done.

"I sent Mrs. Robinson my regards and ended our involvement before I left London." Which confirmed Sophie's note.

"I see," Miranda murmured, not sure that she did, but wanting to say something at his extraordinary revelation. She could not remember such a candid conversation with her husband ever. And there was a part of her, the one she tried to push down, that was quite pleased with the news of the end of the long-term affair between her husband and that woman. "And may I ask what this disturbing news was?"

"Let me just say that it has been handled and is not your concern."

"None of this is my concern, is it, Windmere? I should be ignorant of your business dealings, your personal relationships, all of it. So why do you speak of it now?" So bothered by all he had shared and yet hadn't, she walked to the cabinet and refilled her own glass. "I thought our life had fallen back into its regular pattern since we returned from the Park. Why bother speaking to me about any of this?" She drank down the contents of her glass and poured more.

"I think that you sensed something was different and that you reacted to those changes. Whatever the alteration was between us, I believe it caused me to take certain liberties with you that I would not otherwise have taken."

"Are you apologizing again?" Miranda walked over to him and shook her head. "Have we been separate for so long that you do not remember our time together, Adrian? Certainly, your approach during that night and morning was more ardent than your usual habit, but is that what you are apologizing for?"

"Miranda, a lady, a duchess, should not be exposed to that type of behavior."

She could feel the scream trying to get out from deep inside her. It was filled with anger and terrible words, and she knew she could not let it free. Her misbehaviors had been pointed out to her and she knew he was not offering her a different way of things between them. He was apologizing for making it different those two times.

"I see," she admitted. "So if those times were the aberrations, then you wish to return to our normal schedule?"

"The priority of this marriage remains producing an heir, Miranda, as it always has been."

The words, although she'd been raised and groomed to understand and accept them, stung her. Even though she knew the real purpose of noble marriages was about dynastic succession. Nodding, she swallowed half the brandy in her glass in one mouthful.

"It is as much for your protection as the family and ducal future. I know that sounds harsh, but it is true." He stopped then and drank as though he'd said too much.

Her protection? What did that mean? Her head began swimming from too much brandy in too little time, and she could not focus her thoughts. Rubbing her eyes, she shook her head.

"It is my fault, Windmere. I am not the appropriate wife for a man of your status. I know that. I have known it for some time. You see, for all your mother's strictures and rules and demands for appropriate behavior, she saw it at once, but it was too late to change it. And, of course, my failure to produce the necessary heir efficiently does nothing to raise my esteem in her eyes."

"Miranda? I think you've had too much brandy…." He tried to take the glass from her, but she moved her hand so he could not. Then she drank the rest down.

"If you are being so candid and speaking of such personal things, I can only offer you the same honesty." She brushed her hair back from her face and leaned closer. "Then we must never speak of it again, for such things should never be shared between husband and wife," she said, placing her finger over his lips. "Wait," she said, stumbling over to the decanter, pouring another serving in her glass and turning back to him. "I do not find it as easy as you to be so blunt…."

Miranda knew she was getting drunk, but she simply could not stop herself. It was probably because she was overtired and had had little to eat that day. It was probably also due to the warm, fuzzy feeling it gave her as she tried to face the harsh truth between her husband and herself.

"Miranda! Here now, let me take that." Adrian was suddenly at her side, reaching again for her glass. "I think you've had quite enough." How had he moved that quickly? She blinked and the snifter was gone from her grasp and he was back in his seat.

She walked to her chair and tried to sit in it, but it kept moving. Finally, Adrian took pity on her and pulled her down to it. Well, it was time to be honest with him. Of course, this would not bother him as the information about his mistress had bothered her. He might even be pleased about most of it, for surely it would give him what he wanted most—a decorous wife, who behaved appropriately and at the same time did her best to secure an heir to his dukedom.

"Adrian, I can put up with all of this, most of this, most all of this," she said, waving her hand to make her point. She tried to say the words in her head, but they would not come out the way she wanted.

"I am willing to be your less-than-acceptable wife, one of lower birth who you got stuck with by marrying before you knew about your title." His face turned white but she continued. "I am willing to live in this marriage with nothing more from you than your polite regard and the living you provide to me." She paused, because now he was standing in front of her and she needed to crane her neck to see him. "I am even willing to let go of my dreams of having a husband who loves me and wants me, as my father did my mother."

She stood up now and pressed her finger into his chest. "But I will not lie in my bed while you…you try to secure your heir, and think of my duty, as your mother says I should. I will not lie beneath you and pretend that I am happy. I will not lie still like the cold fish your mother is and act as though I do not want more."

Oh, sweet Jesus! Had she really just said that to him? She clapped her hands over her mouth, but it was too late. Miranda leaned back to see the expression in his eyes, but fell back against the chair instead with her dressing gown tangling around her legs. He wrapped his hands around her arms and pulled her to her feet.

"What do you mean, Miranda? You do not mind the liberties I took? You would welcome them?"

She held her hands tightly over her mouth. She could not admit to more embarrassing truths. She could not....

He lifted her chin and she thought she saw mirth glittering in his hazel-colored eyes. How could a woman not enjoy being naked with a man like this? How could all the wonderful feelings that he could cause with his mouth and his hands and his...body not be something to anticipate? How could she ever lie unmoving again in his embrace as he filled her and made her scream?

Without stopping to wonder if she should or not, Miranda reached up and slid her fingers through his hair, smoothing it into the style he usually wore. Its silky texture tickled her fingers and she wondered what it would feel like on her skin. Pulling his head down, she kissed him, tasting the brandy on his tongue and letting him taste her. Lucky for her, he still held on to her because now, when she opened her eyes, the room spun around. Out of breath, she nodded to him in answer to the question that still circled inside her brain.

"I would welcome them, Adrian. I would."

He kissed her this time and she grabbed the lapels of his evening coat to keep her balance. Well, at least she tried to. Her head seemed to move in one direction, her eyes could not focus, her legs began to tremble and her stomach to spin. Leaning back from Adrian, she shook her head.

"But this is not a good time."

Before she could warn him away, it happened. The Duchess of Windmere cast up her accounts, on the duke, proving that too much of even a very good brandy was not a good thing.

Chapter Eleven

Once again, the punishment inflicted after a breach of the rules proved why the rule existed. Dying, even in the most terrible way imaginable, could not feel this bad. Every movement, every sound caused pain—vibrant, echoing, intensifying pain—in her head. Her stomach twisted in tempo with it and Miranda swore to the Almighty that she would never drink again.

Never.

Ever.

A light pierced the darkness of her room and she clenched her jaws against the pain. What she feared most in that moment happened next.

"Your Grace?" Fisk asked. Even her whispered words slammed into Miranda's head. "His Grace is inquiring about you." A cold cloth placed on her forehead gave her a brief amount of comfort before the weight of it pressed down too much and she flung it away.

"Tell him," she began, and winced at the loudness of her own voice. "Tell him," she whispered, "that Her Grace has died."

His laughter was loud and painful and completely inappropriate for the situation. From the noises his shoes made on the floor, she knew he was walking closer. Miranda prayed she *would* die before he saw how terrible she looked. Lifting her arm to try to cover her face did not work, because nothing in her body answered her commands.

"Although you may feel like dying, Miranda, very few of us actually die from one night's overindulgence." His whisper sounded like a shout.

"Thank you for your kind information, Windmere," she said, trying to open her eyes. They would not respond, either. "One of your shooting pistols would finish this faster and more mercifully."

She felt his touch as he smoothed her hair back from her face, and the cloth, now refreshing and cold, was placed back on her forehead.

"It will pass, Miranda. It will pass." There was some whispering she couldn't understand, and then he kissed her cheek. "Fisk will care for you. I must go out, but I will check on you later."

"Windmere," she called out.

"Yes?"

"I apologize for being sick on your evening clothes."

"Do not think on it, Miranda. Feel better."

Then he was gone, and all she could do was worry

over the parts of their conversation in the study that she could not remember and those she could.

Hours passed before she could open her eyes and sit up in her bed. And a few more hours before her stomach calmed enough for her to sip the remedy sent up by the cook. It was nearly evening before the pounding in her head lessened a sufficient amount so that she did not wince with every noise.

The staff were especially kind—although she knew they all carried out their daily duties, somehow they managed to do it quietly today. She did not ask how they knew of the need for it, but she suspected that everyone knew that the duchess had been drunk as an emperor and tossed up the contents of her stomach on her husband. Well, the embarrassment of facing them would be nothing compared to what she faced with Adrian.

It was nearly nine o'clock when she finally sat before the fire and sipped some of Fisk's special herbal tea. After the beverage stayed quietly in her stomach, Miranda nibbled on a dry biscuit. A soft knock warned her of a visitor and this time it was her husband and not her maid.

"May I visit with you for a few minutes, Miranda?" he asked, peering into her room but not entering it.

"Of course, Windmere." She nodded but regretted the action, which made her head hurt again.

He spoke to someone outside and then closed the door behind him. Walking to where she sat, he wore an expression of concern. His brow crinkled in a frown, but then he smiled.

"Well, your color is certainly better than the last time I saw it. And—" he nodded at the tea and biscuits "—you're able to keep something in your stomach."

"I do apologize again, Windmere. I cannot quite remember the order of events last evening, but I am certain there is no excuse for my drunkenness."

Adrian sat down on the chair next to hers and smiled; it was the knowing smile of someone who had suffered in the same manner himself. "Thompson is the one who may never recover, Miranda. The trousers and stockings are a complete loss."

When she was about to offer another apology, he laughed out loud at her. "I am also certain that he will make do somehow with my others. Now," he said, leaning closer to her and lowering his voice, "how are you feeling? Truly?"

"I am at the point where I believe I might live through it."

"As I said you might." There was a hint of humor in his voice. "My mother sends her regards and hopes that your state of indisposition does not last long."

"Oh, good gracious! I completely forgot!" Miranda dropped the cup noisily onto the table and tossed her napkin aside. Standing, and too quickly at that, only made her head pound furiously until the nausea returned. She clutched her stomach.

How had she forgotten her morning appointment with the dowager? She'd always gone, regardless of her condition, the weather or the situation in the world, when summoned by Adrian's mother. It was easier than facing the endless diatribe that would be her punishment for not appearing on time.

"Miranda! Here, let me help you," Adrian said as he came to her side and guided her back to the chair. "Fisk reminded me of your appointment and I went to my mother's to give your regrets personally. Mother had hoped that your visit to the country at this time of year would have strengthened your constitution."

Miranda looked at him, and the frown and pasty color of her complexion returned. Damn! After experiencing his mother's brand of hospitality for the short time he'd spent there, and after extracting a few truths from her, he had no wonder Miranda dreaded going.

"I explained to her that your regular visits would be discontinued until I said otherwise. Although I know she will miss your company, I made it clear that you had other responsibilities to carry out during the Season."

"I… Windmere…"

Miranda stuttered out a few words but none of them made sense. After discovering that her weekly appointments were no more than excuses for his mother to inspect, berate and embarrass his wife, he'd put a stop to them. How had she endured it without a word of complaint to him? Even worse was the next question—how had he not noticed it?

"If she—beg your pardon, if the dowager—summons you, I want to know about it. You are not to set foot within her home without my express permission."

She gave a start and looked at him now. "Thank you."

As usual between them, she did not argue. But her words, softly spoken, told him things were most likely much worse than he'd been able to discover.

Before he could say anything, a commotion broke out in the corridor and he walked to the door to find out the cause. The household was under orders to keep noise to a minimum in deference to the duchess's illness. Fisk's voice and another woman's rose, and the doorknob turned and twisted as though someone fought to open it against Fisk's wishes. Adrian grabbed the door and pulled on it.

The women spilled in, slamming into him and nearly tumbling them all to the floor. The Viscountess Allendale tried to push past him for the second time this day.

"If you please, Lady Allendale," he said, putting his arm out to stop her progress. "I told you that the duchess is indisposed and not seeing anyone." He would have said more and been more forceful, except that Miranda's hand on his arm and her presence at his side stopped him.

"Sophie," she said. "What is this about?"

Fisk, now back on her feet, stepped to the door to wait. Adrian dismissed her with a nod.

"Miranda, Lady Allendale came by to see you earlier and I told her you were not receiving. Obviously, she has decided not to heed my words." He crossed his arms over his chest, hoping that Miranda's friend understood his displeasure. "This is awfully late to be making a call, Lady Allendale. Do you not have an evening engagement to attend?"

"I am here, Your Grace, due to my concern for Her Grace," she said, glaring at him as though he were some threat to Miranda's well-being. "She, Mir...Her Grace missed the luncheon we had planned for today without a word, and I was worried. My queries, sent here to your house, were returned unopened and unanswered." Then she did the most unladylike thing and crossed her own arms across her chest, challenging him in some way!

"Sophie, I am well," Miranda began, stepping between them. "That is not exactly true, but I am improving." She met his gaze for a moment and then turned to her friend. "Why ever would you think that there is more to this than what Windmere told you earlier?" Her hand rested on his arm, and he wondered if she even realized she was touching him.

"Her Grace has been indisposed, as I mentioned to you, Lady Allendale. But as you can see, she is feeling much better now."

He could sense that there was some reason why Miranda's friend worried over her, but he knew she would never reveal it in front of him. It was time for a strategic retreat.

"Miranda, if you will allow me to escort you back to the chair, I will excuse myself so that you may have a short visit with Lady Allendale." He took her hand and walked her back to the chair closest to the fireplace. Then he turned and glared at Miranda's friend, to make certain she understood his displeasure. Adrian offered a slight bow to both women and then walked to the door, opening it to expose Fisk's presence.

"I will send Fisk to you in a quarter hour, my dear, to help you prepare for bed. I will be in my study if you need me."

He had almost closed the door when she spoke to him. "Windmere?"

Adrian paused and looked at her.

"I am truly grateful for all you've done."

Her words sent shivers through him, ravaging pulses of heat and ice, centering somewhere near his heart, he realized. Her eyes glistened with a hint of tears and her voice trembled as she said the words, leaving him feeling strangely moved.

"Your servant, madam," he said, closing the door. After a word of instruction to Fisk, he went to his study and sent word to Parker to meet him at the club for a late supper.

After waiting what he thought to be an appropriate amount of time without being called back by Miranda, Adrian met Parker as planned. Walking in and accepting a glass of port, he saluted his friend with it as he took a seat next to him in the sitting room of the club.

"I have learned several more things about the duchess," he boasted.

"You certainly apply yourself with vigor to a task when you want to, Windmere," Parker said. "And what have you learned?"

"Several items that cannot be discussed, things of a personal nature, of course," he started, thinking of his mother's true reasons for summoning Miranda and of Miranda's rather adamant admission just before she'd emptied her stomach all over him. "But I do know now that her friend, the termagant, would defend her to the death. If the woman were a man, I might have made a challenge to her over her behavior in my own home."

"Your pardon, Windmere. What termagant are you speaking of? Surely not that chit, Miss Stevenson?" Parker shuddered again, and Adrian wanted to laugh. His friend's discomfort had only just begun.

"No, the Viscountess Allendale. She was nearly intolerable to me. She actually had the nerve to push her way into the duchess's bedchamber! The woman almost knocked me over doing it!"

Parker looked as though he did not believe him. "Allendale seems a likable chap. Too bad to be saddled with a wife like that. Will you speak to him about her behavior?"

Adrian sipped the rich, red port and shook his head. "No. If things go as they may—" he raised an eyebrow to Parker "—Miranda will need her as a friend."

"Ah, I see your meaning," Parker said. He took a mouthful from his own glass and shook his head. "I still find it difficult to believe the news." They sank into a momentary and mutual silence, and Adrian knew they were both thinking of the short future facing him.

"If you are not morose about this, then neither shall I be," Parker said, breaking the silence. "Tell me what you have learned other than the viscountess's deplorable behavior."

"The duchess, although she takes her responsibilities seriously, is still not comfortable being the wife of a duke."

"There's not much to be done about that, Windmere. She *is* the wife of a duke. Oh…I mean to say…" Parker stumbled over his words.

"No offense taken, Parker. This is a strange circumstance to find oneself in."

"Just so." His friend nodded. "Anything else?"

"I learned that the duchess cannot handle brandy and is quite candid and entertaining under its influence. Well, entertaining to a point."

"The duchess was drunk? I mean…"

"Corned, pickled and salted," he replied. It had not been his intent to see her in such a state; indeed, he had not realized how much she'd had until it was too late to make a difference. "Hence her state of indisposition today."

Parker just shook his head. "First that incident by the lake. Now this. Where could this all end?"

Where indeed? The very thought of her admission made Adrian hot with anticipation. These last few years, as he'd heeded the dowager's instructions and taken over control of the rather sizable fortune and power of the estates, and spent more time and attention on his titles, lands and possessions, he'd allowed Miranda to slip away.

He'd believed his mother's words as she made suggestions about delicate matters between him and his wife. Miranda's apparent indifference had seemed to confirm the rightness of his mother's recommendations. He did not want to offend his wife, so he'd found a mistress, *as men of his station did to deal with those more personal needs and affections,* never dreaming of what he was missing in his own bed.

Shaking his head to rid himself of his mother's echoing orders, he looked at Parker. "One can only imagine." Intending to stop the arousing images of Miranda that he knew would fill his mind, Adrian stood. "Before I tell you about the gentleman who has captured Miss Stevenson's fancy, let us find an interesting game of whist for a while."

"Miss Stevenson, you say? Setting her cap for someone this early in the Season? He must have deep pockets." Parker laughed, most likely never realizing that he was the subject in question.

"Although his fortune may not be up to the dowager's usual standards, it is acceptable when coupled with his title. An old, esteemed family from the west of England, she declared."

"Who is the poor sod and can we warn him?" Parker asked as they entered the card room.

Adrian led him to a table. "Too late, I'm afraid. Much too late for that."

And as Adrian had suspected, it was Parker's turn to be corned, pickled and salted when he learned whose name and future was on the dowager's list of potential husbands for her beloved goddaughter.

"You sound terrible," Sophie began. "Let me look at you."

Miranda decided that it hurt less to allow Sophie to have her look. Turning her head this way and that, as slowly as she could, she waited for her friend's pronouncement that she was indeed alive and getting well.

"I have never known you to become so overwrought, Sophie. And so direct with the duke! I had no idea you disliked him so."

"He is the one! I sent polite inquiries asking about you and he returned them. My footman said it was the duke himself and not one of your servants. On my second attempt to contact you, he turned my message to Fisk away." Sophie was not one to be easily dissuaded. "Then, he refused me permission to enter this afternoon."

"I appreciate your efforts on my behalf, but, as you can now see, I am fine." Miranda pointed to the chair next to hers. "Please sit a few minutes and calm yourself. If you are this upset, I am certain that your husband noticed and must be worrying, too."

"John? No, he is fine," Sophie explained. "He knows how I am when…" Her words stopped and she made a choking sound.

"You are in the family way once more?"

Sophie nodded.

"My felicitations on such joyful news, and I apologize for being a source of concern for you when you should be thinking about other things."

Another baby for Sophie. Her husband was ecstatic over it, Miranda was certain. She swallowed against her own disappointment and offered a smile to her friend.

"Oh, Miranda," Sophie cried, "I did not want you to find out this way. I know how much you want a child. I should never have come here this evening." She tugged a handkerchief from her reticule. "But I worried that my advice had again caused problems for you."

"Your counsel is always appreciated, Sophie. I did follow it, but the results were not what you likely expected them to be."

"I promise to offer no more advice on the subject of your marriage. I told John that I cannot bear knowing that I made your life unhappier because I thought to instruct you. Goodness! If I continue, soon I will be no better than the dowager."

"I would like to put your mind at rest," Miranda said. "Although what happened was an unusual series of events, I believe that Windmere and I have come to some type of understanding."

"You have?" Sophie asked while dabbing at her eyes. "You settled whatever happened on your recent trip to Windmere Park, then?"

"I believe we have."

"You *believe* you have? Is there some concern still left unsettled? Did you speak your mind to him?"

Miranda looked away.

"What did you mean when you called it an 'unusual series of events'? Did he…? In some way…? Did you…?"

It was better to put this to rest before Sophie became more upset. "The forthright and frank discussion we had last evening was unexpected. I was restless and sought out a bit of brandy, and Windmere was doing the same."

"And? You had some brandy…. Oh, dear! Miranda, you cannot drink brandy! You have no tolerance of the stuff."

"I confess that I did not think about that. I overindulged while we spoke, and I think that Windmere was as much surprised by the topic of discussion as he was by the contents of my stomach when they covered him."

Sophie shuddered. "Ah, I see it now. Your illness today is the result of the brandy."

"Yes. And Windmere has been the absolute gentleman in this, even going to the dowager's appointment for me."

"He didn't!" Sophie exclaimed.

"I can only think that he discovered the whole of it, for he has forbidden me to visit there without him."

Miranda sat back after revealing the incredible command Adrian had made. Did he have any idea of how much it meant to her? Did he know the dowager's intentions at those morning appointments?

"There may be hope here, after all."

"Hope for what, Sophie? He has removed the most unpleasant thing I have to do as his wife. That is all there

is to this," she said. Of course, if any of what she thought
she might have said or done actually transpired, there
might be one or two other changes between them.

"If he did not care, why would he have troubled himself to make things even more difficult between himself
and his mother? Surely…" Sophie paused and shook her
head. "No, I cannot proceed with this. Every time I do,
you suffer for it."

"Nonsense, Sophie. I value your concern and the fact
that we can speak of things that I cannot share with another person. Now, I am feeling overtired and I am sure
that you must need your rest, as well." Miranda stood
and called out for Fisk. "I heard my husband's carriage
leave a few minutes ago, so you do not have to worry
over seeing him on your way out."

Sophie walked to the door with her. "If you are feeling up to it, perhaps you could call tomorrow? A new
circulating library opened last week on Bond Street and
I would love to visit it."

"I would like that also. And if I do not feel up to it,
I will send word to you so that you do not worry."

"Please offer my apologies to the duke for my regrettable behavior? I will send him a note, but he may tear
it to bits without reading it."

Fisk opened the door and a footman waited to escort
Sophie out. Miranda waved the servants out for a moment and closed the door to give them some privacy.
Unable to stop herself, she threw her arms around Sophie and hugged her.

No one had cared about her well-being since her father died. Oh, Adrian, his mother and others showed concern, but that concern was also based on their need or expectations of her, and not about the person inside. Only Sophie did, and it warmed Miranda's heart to know that her friend would do battle with a duke and a formidable maid to get to her.

"Thank you for worrying about me, Sophie. It means so much to me," she said, squeezing her friend tightly. The tears flowed as she held on. Finally, she took a deep breath and released her. "Now we're both watering pots." Reaching in the pocket of her dressing gown, she withdrew a handkerchief and dried her eyes.

"I am always here for you, Miranda, and I know you would do the same for me."

"Now, before Lord Allendale calls for a runner to find you, let me send you on your way home." Pulling open the door, she stepped aside.

The footman led the way, and Miranda asked Fisk to follow in case Sophie needed anything before leaving. Turning back to her room, she tried to make herself feel the happiness she'd professed for her friend's news. All her strength left her in that moment and she dragged herself to her bed and lay on it, not bothering to pull the covers down.

Tired from being ill, tired from too much brandy and tired from all the emotions of the last few weeks, Miranda pushed it all away and tried to fall asleep. She would try to fulfill her duties to Adrian and to his family with good cheer, accepting the good fortune she had in such a marriage. Even if she knew she was a fraud and a failure, she would not let it show.

Chapter Twelve

He endured four musicales, twelve afternoon calls, two formal balls, a night at Almack's, three morning rides on Rotten Row, and five late suppers out, with another planned in his own house a few days hence. He danced with her, he paired up with her to play cards, he turned the sheets as she played the piano at one gathering, and attended a salon at which the classics were read and discussed. They went to the theater and to Vauxhall for the fireworks and amusements there.

He watched her from near and from afar and took in everything about her that he could. From the foods she ate to the clothes she wore, he took note of everything. She liked the morning best and preferred simpler, plainer foods to more exotic ones. Her favorite fragrance was a light floral one with a hint of citrus and some other spice he could not identify.

Whether on purpose or by accident, she did not fill the house with flowers, but preferred watercolors and other paintings to offer color and brightness to their abode. The biggest surprise to him was her own abilities with watercolors. Some of the most appealing ones he found in a storage room turned out to be hers, and, to her obvious embarrassment, he insisted that they be displayed.

He discussed much of what he discovered with Parker, who offered some rather sound observations and assisted him in making some arrangements for her. And when the spells came over him, on an increasing basis, Parker helped him. Adrian thought that Miranda had become aware of the more frequent coughing, too, but she never mentioned it.

The solicitor finalized the plans he'd outlined, and Webb was put on the task of securing a house in Bath and one in Brighton, since the physicians and Mrs. Gresham had all recommended taking the waters and a stay near the seashore to improve his health. He had not told Miranda of that yet, but he suspected that she would agree to leave London on any excuse.

Finally, just over a week after the incident that ruined his favorite shoes, Adrian decided that there was only one thing he was avoiding and, if there was to be any hope of protecting Miranda's future with a child, it was time to visit her bed again. There was more to it than that, but with everything he was handling, it was easier to keep the fraying threads of his life woven together by keeping things as unemotional as possible.

For Miranda's protection, they needed a son.

Simple. Clear. True.

They were waltzing after a supper at Lord and Lady Allendale's house, where Miranda's friend had hosted a not-quite-intimate party of thirty, when he took the chance. Adrian allowed his hand to slide over her waist a bit more than would be acceptable between strangers, and she met his gaze. Beads of sweat gathered on his back and he began to feel like an untried youth rather than the many-years-married man he was.

He watched the sparkle in her eyes as they swirled around the dance floor, and inhaled her scent as they moved together. If it were possible, he thought that she felt it, too, for her breathing changed—not in pace with the steps, but a bit halting each time their eyes met. Her body felt warmer and softer in his arms as the music grew louder and more intense. He cleared his throat.

"May I escort you home, Miranda?" he asked.

This time, unlike that other waltz, she did not falter in her steps or hesitate in his arms. Watching her face for signs of acceptance or rejection, he almost tripped himself when he saw the tip of her tongue slide out to moisten her lips.

"Of course, Windmere," she said. She gazed at him and smiled. "I would like that."

He hardened in that moment, unable to think of anything but getting her home and peeling off the layers of clothing that hid her from his sight and touch. Perhaps taking separate coaches was a safer idea? Adrian did not know if he had the restraint to keep his hands off her on the way.

They must have finished the dance, for he did not remember making a scene by dragging his wife off the floor. They must have offered their farewells to their host and hostess, and someone must have called for the carriage. He remembered none of it. After helping her into it, Adrian stared out of the window, clenching his hands into fists to keep from touching her and from allowing the desire that had been building between them to explode in a carriage.

Now, he stepped onto the street, assisted Miranda out and then up the steps and in the door. Adrian knew that he needed to slow down or he was in danger of creating another debacle that seemed to be linked to making love with his wife. No matter how well trained, well paid or well known for their discretion his servants were, he suspected that they would take offense at the sight of the master and mistress of the house in flagrante delicto.

A sense of urgency seemed to fill the house as they walked up the stairs to their chambers. Miranda did not say a word, but he could tell she was breathless. He hoped and prayed that it was a good sign. His body wanted to make her scream, but that would happen soon enough.

He paused at her door and Fisk opened it from inside, ready to do her mistress's bidding. Miranda turned to say something, but he stopped her with his finger on her lips.

"No more than a quarter hour, Miranda."

He took a step away and then pulled her into his arms and kissed her, taking her mouth in a hungry approximation of what his body wanted to do. Rather than standing rigid in his embrace, she softened in his arms, melting against him and urging his body and him to more blatant actions. He pressed his hardness against her and moved his hips so she could feel his condition.

"Ten minutes, no more," he whispered roughly.

If she had held back, he could have walked away, but the soft moan that escaped her broke his control, and he walked them into her dressing room. "Get out," he ordered, and Fisk had the good sense to leave, and quickly. When the door closed, he lifted his head and looked at his wife.

"I fear I have waited too long, Miranda. I will try not to do anything that will necessitate an apology in the morning."

"As will I, Windmere."

She smiled and he laughed, kissing her openmouthed and pulling out the pins that held her hair in an elaborate arrangement. It might have been easier if Fisk had undressed her, but Adrian had imagined removing each layer until he uncovered her willing flesh…and then covered it with his body. Much more fun for him and an early night for the duchess's maid.

Miranda lifted her hands behind her head to assist him, and instead, it inflamed his desire. Did she not realize how the action raised her breasts to almost overflowing the low neckline of her gown? Could she not see how much he wanted to taste the wonderfully pebbled tips and suck them until she screamed? They were already held enticingly high by her corset, and with a slight move of his hand, he could have them free.

He released her and she took a step away, shaking her head until her hair flowed down her back in thick, golden-brown waves. In contrast with the gown she wore, she looked like a garden nymph with her large blue eyes and flowing locks.

He wanted her. He wanted her badly.

"It would kill me if you lay beneath me as before and did not find pleasure in this, Miranda," he admitted. "I can make this good for you if you permit me to," he whispered as he kissed down her neck and ever closer to her breasts.

"Windmere," she said, whispering in turn.

"I would have honesty between us in this, Miranda. I expect you to stop me if something does not please you, or offends you in any way. I fear my desire for you has me past the point where my attentions will be mannerly and controlled."

"Should I anticipate forceful attentions then, Windmere?"

"If you call me Adrian, I can guarantee them. But only if you want them. Tell me, Miranda. Tell me what you want."

She hesitated, afraid to let him know how much he had stirred her own desire these last days and hours and minutes. He did remember the words she'd said while drunk, especially about their marital relations. And now he wanted her. Each time in the past, any attempt on her part to reach for more, to make their marriage better in some personal way, had failed. Did she have the courage to take what she wanted in this?

"I will not lie quietly beneath you, Adrian. I do not want this to be a duty between us any longer," Miranda said, as she searched his face for a reaction. When his body surged against her, and he rubbed the proof of his desire against her belly, she whispered his name. "Adrian…"

Instead of the onslaught of kisses she expected, he stood and stared at her with an intensity she'd not seen in him before. His hands inched down to the bottom of her skirts and he raised them slowly, allowing his fingers to glide over her as he did. She followed his lead, raising her hands and arms so that he could ease the dress over her head. Once it was gone, he leaned down and kissed the valley of her breasts until she felt them swell under his attentions. Her hands drifted to his head and she ran her own fingers through his silky curls.

Just when her legs threatened to give way, he scooped her up in his arms and carried her through the doorway to her bedroom, dropping her shoes along the way. Instead of stopping, he continued into his own room and kicked the door closed with his foot.

She had only been here in passing and never in his bed. The smell of the polished mahogany of the bed and closet and other furniture pervaded the room, but it was the scent of the spicy cologne he always wore that enticed her now. When he reached the side of the bed, he paused, lowering her to her feet and wrapping himself around her.

His hands slid around her waist as he sought out the ties of her corset. When he lost the battle, he slipped his fingers in the front, where her breasts were straining against the whalebone and fabric, and lifted them free. She could not help the sigh that escaped as he caressed them.

"Adrian," she whispered, as his touch aroused the tips into hard buds. She braced her hands on his shoulders and clutched his jacket.

His mouth was hot when it touched her skin. His tongue slid over her breasts and then back up to her neck. She felt his teeth graze the sensitive curl of her ear and she shivered as a thrill passed through her. He kissed her then, tasting her mouth as he had her skin. Stepping back, he tugged off his jacket, waistcoat, and pulled his cravat loose. When he began to unbutton his shirt and the flaps of his trousers, she thought she understood the meaning of that new process, mesmerization.

Unable to move, unable to think, she could only watch as he tossed aside one piece of clothing after another until he stood before her naked. His chest and stomach were sprinkled with dark hair that continued down below his waist.

Miranda hesitated to look there, but her gaze was caught by his maleness. Surprising her, he turned and strode to a cabinet and pulled open a drawer. She watched the muscles of his thighs flex as he walked, and she ached to touch him. He came back with a pair of scissors, looking intent on committing some kind of damage. Taking her shoulders, he spun her around and she felt the corset loosen immediately.

"Damn laces!" he muttered, as he cut through the ties holding the corset together. Triumphant, he threw the sections of her undergarment aside and brought her back to face him. Now that she was in only her chemise and stockings, her rosy-tipped breasts tempted him once more. Somehow he managed to lift and remove the chemise before taking her in his arms and feeling the heat of her explode against his skin.

He knew that he would be unable to slow their pace down now that he'd sampled her. Moving a step at a time, he soon had her against the bed. Lifting her onto it, he allowed her a moment to move back from the edge before kneeling between her legs. She sat silently as he undid each of her stockings from the garters that held them, and rolled them down over her calves, ankles and feet.

Her breathing changed, growing more erratic, and her eyes closed as he caressed her legs, grazing the skin with the tips of his fingers, up over her sensitive knees, onto her thighs. As he touched the soft hair there, she gasped and whispered his name again. Feeling for the tender flesh, he found her warm and soft and wet... ready for him.

Adrian watched her face as he entered her tight

sheath and pushed forward until he touched the very center of her. Leaning on his elbows, he took her hands, entwined their fingers and held them above her head. She panted as though running as he filled her and withdrew, over and over until he thought he was close to finding release.

Her body tightened around his hardness, telling him that she was as close as he was, and he kissed her on the mouth, sliding his tongue inside to tease hers. She arched against him and moaned as he moved deeper inside of her. He smiled. Regardless of sensibilities and misunderstandings, her body welcomed him and everything he did to her. The tension within him grew and he moved faster and faster, seeking not only the satisfaction he knew was moments away, but also something more that only she could give him.

He released her hands and he felt her slide them down his back, urging him on. Adrian felt his release begin and the words spilled into his mind even as his seed spilled inside his wife.

For…

For…

The words he chanted in his thoughts each time he bedded her, the prayers for a successful outcome, faded, and all he could utter was her name.

"Miranda," he moaned, as he plunged inside and allowed them both to fall over the precipice to satisfaction. "Miranda."

It was some time later, when their breathing eased,

that he turned on his side and tugged her closer. Miranda did not resist, but moved into his embrace, fitting her back against his front. Although he could not stop touching her, he soon realized that she was dozing.

Adrian thought about her response to him, the way her body blossomed at his touch and the way she sighed his name. She rarely used it and he found that he liked the sounds of it on her lips. Not used to hearing it, for not many called him by his Christian name, he found the way she dragged it out aroused him.

He also enjoyed the way she leaned against him, snuggling deeper in his embrace, in her sleep. Reaching down for a sheet, he covered them with it and lay just listening to her breaths, coming regularly now.

Had they been successful this night? Would she ever bear a child? He was not sure if the problem was hers or, possibly due to his health, his. It was a frightening thought, but he realized that in the years during which he'd bedded both his wife and his mistress with some regularity, neither had conceived.

Certainly, Caro was a more experienced woman and, most likely, used some preventative method to avoid conception. But Miranda's duty was to produce an heir, and he doubted she knew of ways to prevent pregnancy. He looked over to the wooden box on top of his bureau that carried all of the herbs and medicaments he used. Mrs. Gresham had alluded to there being a number of possible side effects of all the concoctions he took, and had warned him of several.

Miranda stirred in his arms and he knew he should return her to her own room. By now, the tea brewed for imbibing at bedtime grew cold in his dressing room, but he needed to drink it nonetheless. Physical strain, even of the amorous kind, seemed to increase the tightness in his lungs and the urge to cough. He slid his arm out from under her head and moved away from her, careful not to wake her yet. Putting on his smalls, he walked to the door of the dressing room and opened it as quietly as he could. He wasn't surprised when Thompson entered immediately from the hall to see to his needs.

After a few instructions to his valet, Adrian drank down the tepid tea and gave the cup back. Then he opened the wooden case and took out the flask and drank from it, hoping to loosen his chest. Mrs. Gresham's elixir was more successful than any of the previous ones given him by the physicians, and it did not sour his stomach as many of theirs did. Adrian closed and locked the cabinet and turned back to the bed. Miranda lay there observing his every move.

"Your lung condition worsens?" she asked. Pushing her hair over her shoulders, she sat up and slid back against the pillows and headboard. He looked lost for words and a bit sheepish, as though caught at something he did not want seen.

"It varies from time to time," he said, walking toward her. "The physicians say it is simply the change in seasons."

Something in his tone or expression told her there

was more to this that he did not wish to reveal. The nonchalance he affected did not cover all his concern. She remembered hearing several outbreaks of coughing while they were at Windmere Park, and at least one other here.

"Is there ought that can be done? You have seen the physicians?"

"I have seen them, as recently as last month," he said. "Their recommendations included carrying out my normal activities and leaving the city when the heat and smoke in the air are at their worst." Reaching the bed, he crawled back into it, sliding in next to her. The thin linen of his small clothes did nothing to mask his intent. "I am to avoid those substances that cause my cough to worsen, such as feathers and hay."

"So that is why, even though you ride often, you never enter the stables."

"Just so. My grooms know to wipe down a horse before bringing it to me. And the housekeeper has made pillows stuffed with cloth and not feathers."

Miranda realized that was the reason his bedding felt different from hers—there was no feather-stuffed pillow top on his mattress and not as much puffiness to his pillows.

"And that is enough? The doctors are in agreement with the prognosis for your health?" she asked.

"My health is quite fine, thank you. And," he said as he reached for her and pulled her against him, "they said that a strong appetite is a sign of health."

She laughed at his overt attempt at a double enten-
dre. When she would have questioned him further about
what the physicians had told him, he slid his arms
around her from behind. As he held her tightly against
his chest and placed her bottom as though she sat on his
lap, his other hand slipped between her thighs and found
that sensitive spot that made her ache.

Adrian moved his fingers, finding the moisture already there and causing more. Miranda gasped with
each deep caress and he became relentless in his actions.
Just as she felt everything within her tighten and as the
excitement within her grew, he lifted her leg and entered
her from behind.

The pleasurable sensations, with his fingers still there
teasing her from the outside and now his hardness filling her inside, grew until it threatened to erupt. Aching
and throbbing, she found each movement of her hips
brought either his fingers or his hardness into closer
contact, and it was driving her mad.

"Adrian," she called out. "Adrian, help me!"

Then she was truly lost, for all of the pleasure and
aching and throbbing exploded and she could hear herself scream as he continued his attention to the places
that ached the most for release. Her body convulsed as
wave after wave shuddered through her. Just as she
thought herself finished, he kissed her neck and then bit
the sensitive skin on her shoulder, bringing another
wave of release to her and, this time, to him. Adrian
thrust deeper and held her still as he poured into her.

Out of breath and still held in his arms, she thought she may have lost consciousness for a moment as her body continued to pulse and throb. He embraced her while she slowly calmed, and did not loosen his hold until she let out a final sigh of pleasure.

She drifted off to sleep then, completely satisfied and exhausted by his forceful attentions. When she woke, most of the morning was gone and she was in her own bed. Her body, overwhelmed by her husband's demands, ached in places a proper duchess did not think about. Miranda smiled. It was a Friday morning, and thanks to Adrian, she did not dread the day.

Stretching under the covers, she felt the sheets brush across her still-sensitive breasts, and shivered. Not only had they shared a pleasurable encounter, he had twice more applied his attentions to her in the night—the second time in his bed and the third when he carried her back to her room. She could have walked had they not been...not been...well, engaged in marital relations at the time.

The heat of a blush filled her cheeks as she thought about that. She did not remember the beginning of it, except that he had taken something she said as some kind of challenge, and the next thing she knew, his hands held her bottom and her legs were wrapped around his hips as they moved from his room to hers.

Was this what men did with their mistresses? Did they reserve this lighthearted approach only for women they paid for the privilege of sharing a bed? Or was this simply what she and Adrian had been missing because of their attempts to be the proper duke and duchess? Although she and Sophie never discussed the particulars, Miranda suspected that the Allendales found much happiness in their marriage bed. Even though the royal princes were probably not a good example of how the upper classes behaved, she doubted that every man with a title had a bit o' muslin tucked away.

Time would tell if Adrian's interest would continue to be as ardent as the night before or if this was a passing fancy of his after discovering that she would accept such advances from him. Although warned severely and often by the dowager that proper wives did not allow such behavior, Miranda hoped to be both to him—a proper wife and one who attracted him to her bed. Now that she understood what the dowager must have been missing in her life, Miranda was determined to have a different marriage than that.

Of course, the last time she'd allowed herself to hope about this subject was after she'd become completely and utterly pickled. Well, the experience of discussing her husband's mistress with him and making some rather personal disclosures of her own was more the cause of the drinking binge than her hope. And since then, he'd definitely been more attentive to her, showing up when least expected at balls and dinners and musicales. Even joining in the escort of Miss Stevenson at his mother's request.

The tiny flame of optimism still burned within Miranda's heart. Perhaps there was a chance for them to have a marriage like her parents'. Perhaps in time Adrian would come to cherish her in some small way—not love, of course, but something warm and affectionate that would feel like love.

Perhaps in time.

Chapter Thirteen

"Has the dowager told you of any others who seem interested in the chit's hand yet?"

Adrian sat down in the drawing room of his club and perused the morning edition of the *Gazette,* completely ignoring Parker's nagging. His friend had been seated next to Miss Stevenson at another supper party last evening and was beginning to feel the pressure. Parker did not want to admit in so many words that he found her company pleasurable or that he was not opposed to thinking about marriage. For a moment he followed Adrian's example and picked up a copy of the newspaper, but proved to have little patience this morning.

"Blast it, Windmere! My parents are making all the noises about her, too!" he exclaimed, tossing the paper aside.

"Feeling the parson's noose tightening, Parker?"

Adrian laughed. "It is about time for you to think about setting up a nursery, after all."

The words slipped out of his mouth—the usual and necessary reason for marriage—and he thought yet again about how much he wanted to fill his own nursery. Even if he was not here to see the child grow, at least it would fulfill one of the most important responsibilities to his family. Miranda showed no signs of increasing in spite of the additional nights he spent in her bed. Though he'd been handling all the important matters of his life, it was still his one regret.

"Is there someone else you have a fancy for, Parker? Or is it just that Miss Stevenson does not fit what you're looking for in a wife?"

"More likely I fear the closeness to the dowager, Windmere. I cannot imagine going through life saddled with her as nearly my mother-by-marriage. I know she would not be the real thing. After all, Juliet's—pardon, Miss Stevenson's—own mother still lives. But the situation would be too close for comfort." Parker shuddered, much like Adrian did when he thought about his mother's interference.

"So, tell me what you hope for in a wife and perhaps I can be looking for one for you. We both have vouchers for next week, so we could begin hunting in earnest then." He was teasing Parker, but the man was so nervous over the topic that he did not realize the fact.

They paused as one of the servers brought over coffee and cakes, and then Parker stretched out his legs and nodded. "An excellent idea! First, I want a woman without pretensions, who doesn't put on airs."

"A woman of humility?" he asked.

"Just so. My family does have several estates, not as large and significant as yours, Windmere, but a responsibility all the same. I want a woman able to live in the country or in the city with the same ease."

"A country mouse and a city mouse, then?"

"An apt description. Next, I would like my wife to be a companion to me, and so I want her to enjoy some of my favorite pastimes."

"Betting on the horses, drinking that single malt I introduced you to and spending an occasional hour with…what is her name? At Madame Beverley's School of Venus?"

"Windmere, we are speaking of a wife now!" Parker looked around to see if others were listening in on their conversation. Content that none were, he leaned over and spoke sotto voce. "Of course, I would certainly like a woman who looks with favor on, shall we call them, 'the activities of the night'? The last thing I want is some missish young thing who cries at the thought of it."

Adrian's thoughts drifted off to the qualities that Parker had listed. All of the attributes that his friend looked for were a perfect description of Adrian's own wife. When had Parker fallen in love with Miranda? Did Parker even know?

"No, Windmere, the pastimes I was referring to were

an occasional card game, listening to music, perhaps even a game of billiards or some archery."

Adrian's mouth dropped open now. Shaking his head, he could not believe Parker would be so blatant about his attraction to Miranda. Or that he, her own husband, had completely missed all signs of it.

"Do you realize what you are saying, Parker? Do you realize who the woman is that you are describing?"

"I thought this was just conjecture? I do not believe I mentioned someone in particular, although I think Miss Stevenson might be close on several of those points." Parker drank his coffee and placed the cup on a passing server's tray. Wiping his mouth, he frowned at Adrian. "Tell me, who do *you* think it is?"

"Miranda appears to fit your description of the perfect wife!" he growled through clenched teeth.

"Windmere! I am not the kind of man who dawdles with another man's wife! If there appears to be any correlation between the traits I want in my future wife and your present one, I do apologize." Pulling his handkerchief from his pocket, he dabbed at his face. "Truly."

Jealousy tore at Adrian's gut. Not that he suspected anything was going on between Parker and Miranda, but the thought of someone else wanting her, loving her, touching her, sent his anger soaring. She was *his* wife, even if only for a few more months.

Then she would be his widow.

Alone, on her own. He would not be there to live with

her. He would not be there to touch her or to laugh or dance with her. Adrian would not be there to love her.

Bloody hell…he was in love with his wife.

The shock of it must have shown on his face, for Parker began calling loudly for a glass of whisky, which he placed in Adrian's hand with all haste. After tossing down the first one quickly, then a second, Adrian stopped. Although he wanted more, he knew the consequences of trying to drown this kind of revelation with liquor.

The worst part was the rest of it.

After discovering this new relationship with her, Adrian knew she needed it to thrive. Without it she would shrivel and dry up, like so many women whose usefulness was done. She'd mentioned once on that night weeks ago when she'd gotten drunk that she had given up her dream of having a marriage like her parents' had been. That she was willing to live with a polite but unloving husband.

Now he knew that a house and an income would be important, but not as much as finding her someone she could love. Miranda needed someone to take care of her heart and soul. Miranda needed…a new husband, who would give her the love she needed and wanted after Adrian was gone.

The pain nearly cut him in two, forcing him to buckle over. The whisky glass went flying and his chest constricted. Adrian tried to reach for his flask, but he couldn't find it in his pocket. Even as his breathing grew more difficult, he tried to clear his thoughts and let the air move into his lungs on its own.

Too late. As he saw the horrified faces of those witnessing the attack, he wondered if this was the one that would end his life.

It could not. He still had too many things to do.

He needed to find a new husband for Miranda. He had to find…

"We've sent for a physician, Windmere," he heard Parker say as he was eased down onto a couch. "Try to breathe."

The darkness swirled and invaded until he could hear nothing and see nothing. He prayed once more as he faded, the words coming easily to his mind now. He reached out to Parker and tugged him close so that only he would hear the words.

"We must find a new husband for Miranda." Parker pulled away. The light faded and the only thing Adrian could see was her face. "For Miranda."

It was nearly two days and nights later when he came to himself again. Darkness and light, murmured words and orders, soft crying and worried whispers filled his mind. His body, racked with pain now, hurt when he moved, but most especially when he tried to take a deep breath. He tried reaching up to wipe his face, but realized someone held his hand at his side. Forcing his eyes to open, he turned and saw the cause.

Miranda sat at his side with her fingers entwined with

his. She was half sitting, half reclining in the chair, sound asleep. When he tried to loosen her hand, she tightened her grasp and mumbled something in her sleep. The noise was enough to alert Thompson, who peeked in the slightly opened door and saw that he was awake.

"Your Grace," the valet said, bowing to him. "'Tis a good thing to see you awake."

"It does not feel good, Thompson," he whispered back. "How long has Her Grace been like this?"

"The duchess finally fell asleep about an hour ago," Thompson replied, as he stepped closer. "Her Grace has not left your side since she fought her way in and threw the others out. That was very late last evening."

"Thompson, get me a glass of something cold to drink and then I want the details. Hurry, but do not disturb the duchess's rest."

She must need it, for there were black smudges beneath her eyes and she looked exhausted. Her hair was pulled back from her face, but hung in tangles. He glanced at what she wore and was horrified to see all sorts of marks and stains on her gown. Miranda looked more like a scullery maid than the lady of the house.

Thompson was back directly, but when Adrian reached out for the cup of tea, he could not hold it steady in his hand. His grip was so weak that Thompson finally guided him. With one hand behind Adrian's head and one on the cup, his valet aided him in drinking the brew. The coolness of it soothed his dry throat and he nodded in thanks.

"Now, what happened?"

"Well, Your Grace, word reached us that you had taken ill and were being brought back here for care. Lord Parker arrived with you, but you were unconscious. The dowager wasn't two steps behind you and she took over, ordering possets and concoctions and sending word to her own physician to come immediately. The household was in an uproar by the time the doctor got here."

"And Her Grace? Where was she?" Adrian asked.

"I don't know where the duchess was when you were taken ill, but she arrived back here some hours later, never knowing what had happened to you."

"My mother…the dowager never sent word to her?"

"No, Your Grace. Lord Parker is the one that finally found her and sent her word."

Adrian paused and asked for more of the tea. His throat was scratchy, as though he'd been yelling. After taking a few more sips, he nodded to Thompson to continue.

"Lord Parker told her what had happened, and how the dowager wouldn't allow him in and was having the surgeon let your blood—twice. I didn't know that a person could turn the color the duchess did—no offense intended to Her Grace, of course."

If he had not felt so poorly, he might enjoy this story. Adrian took another mouthful of tea and then waited to hear more.

"The duchess pushed her way in here and carried on like that Lady Allendale did that night? I can't be sure, but there could have been a swear word or two bandied about before she tossed the surgeon, the dowager's physician and servants out."

"Miranda threw my mother out?" And he'd missed such an event?

"Actually, Your Grace, the duchess said the dowager could wait here or at her own domicile for you to awaken. They'd given you laudanum to quiet you down."

Laudanum explained the headache and dry mouth. "My mother left?" Astounded, Adrian chuckled. If only he could have witnessed the scene.

"No, Your Grace," Thompson whispered. "The duchess took her by the arm and 'helped' her down the stairs and out the door to her carriage when the dowager said she would wait here, in your room."

And his mother went because to do otherwise would break her own rules about impeccable behavior. "And Lord Parker?"

"Lord Parker is asleep on the couch in the sitting room. 'Guarding the door against dragons and other possible dangers' were his words."

Adrian did manage a laugh then. Although he quieted immediately, Miranda stirred. She opened her eyes, startled for moment, as though she did not remember where she should be, and then focused on him.

"Adrian," she whispered. Then, spotting Thompson nearby, she blushed. "Pardon my lapse, Windmere."

He lifted her hand to his mouth and kissed her knuckles. "I am certain that Thompson was not offended by it."

"How do you feel? Can you breathe now? Does it still pain you?"

Question followed question as she sought answers, until she stopped and burst into tears. He drew her closer until he could wrap his arms around her. That was when he saw the bandages around his lower arms, where the bloodletting had been performed. He could not hold her as tightly as he'd like to, but he rubbed his hand over her back, trying to ease her fear.

"I am well enough, Miranda. Please stop crying and talk to me."

She sat up and looked for something to dry her eyes with. Thompson was there with a handkerchief, and then stepped discreetly away once more. When it appeared that she was about to cry again, Adrian smiled at her.

"I heard that you put Lady Allendale's behavior to shame."

"You know, Windmere, you should not hold that one lapse against her forever. She was worried about me."

"Dare I hope that you worried over me?"

She tried to smile but could not. Tears filled her eyes again and he cursed himself for his lame attempt at humor. She dropped her head down on his shoulder and cried. Adrian looked around to get Thompson's help and found his valet returning with Fisk in tow.

"Ah, Fisk, can you help with the duchess? She is overwrought." An understatement, but the servants knew better than he the nervous tension and constant worry his wife had been subjected to by his sudden illness.

"Come, Your Grace. Let me help you to your room," Fisk murmured. "His Grace wants you to rest now."

Miranda looked to him and he nodded. "Thompson is going to help me clean up, Miranda. I will send for you when I finish."

She stared down at her own gown and nodded, as though realizing for the first time how disheveled she was. Miranda allowed Fisk to assist her out of the room.

He spoke her name before the door shut. "Miranda?" She looked at him and waited. "My thanks for your tender care," he said.

She nodded and was gone. Within a few minutes, an army of servants were filing in and out of his room, changing his bedclothes, mopping the floor, bringing in buckets of steaming water for a bath and seeing to every need he might have. It was exhausting, and he found himself drifting off after just a few minutes in the tub.

Adrian allowed Thompson to do the brunt of the work cleaning up his appearance, and then asked that Lord Parker be summoned. Thompson was just helping him back into bed when his friend entered the room.

"A bit of a rough day, eh, Windmere?"

Adrian dismissed Thompson for the night and turned to his friend. "I have much to thank you for, Will. I would probably be dead if not for you."

"It was the duchess who saved you, Adrian. I was only the messenger."

"Regardless," he said, clearing his now tight throat,

"your quick action at the club and then making certain that Miranda was here are the reasons I am still breathing."

"I have heard you cough, but never heard anything like that," Parker said. "I do not think I understood the seriousness of your condition until yesterday. Is that how it will happen?"

"Apparently. The physicians say that each attack like this one damages the tissues, and that there will be one attack when I will simply not be able to take any air into my lungs."

"You have seemed much better lately. Mrs. Gresham's tonics appeared to be working. Now this."

Adrian knew the cause of this attack. Emotional or nervous tension made him more vulnerable, and he'd just had the most incredible epiphany about his feelings for Miranda. Then he'd crashed from the highest of emotions to the lowest as he'd realized he would need to find someone to take care of her after he was gone.

"Ah, speaking of Mrs. Gresham…" Parker began, looking somewhat embarrassed.

"What about her?"

"I was so upset by your attack that I may have shared her name with the duchess. Only for your own good, of course."

"The duchess or the dowager?" He did not want his mother privy to his treatments. One moment in charge and look what she'd allowed.

"The duchess. Your wife."

But she would be someone else's wife after his death.

No, he was not ready to contemplate that issue at the moment.

"I will release you from your duty as protector now. Give me a day or two and I shall need to speak with you about another matter." Adrian held out his hand to his friend. Parker shook it and nodded, promising to return as requested.

Adrian slid down into the comfort of his bed and found himself drifting off to sleep, but an hour or two later he roused. Restless now, he stumbled out of his bed and found his way into Miranda's room. Using the footboard as a support, he stood and watched her sleeping.

With her hair loose and the tension gone from her face, she looked younger. The smudges were still under her eyes, but, hopefully, rest would take care of those. Never would he think that she'd take on his mother and win, and on his behalf. Never would he think that she'd care enough even to intercede, but she had.

Miranda moaned and tossed a bit as though struggling in her sleep. When she spoke his name, he found himself at her side. He lifted the bedcovers and climbed in next to her. Without hesitation and without waking, she moved into his embrace and wrapped her body around his.

He smoothed her hair away from her face and kissed her forehead. "Shh, Miranda. All is well now," he whispered as he settled next to her.

He listened to her breathing as he held her close. Every part of him hurt—his chest, his head, his arms—

but for once, his heart did not. No longer empty, he knew without a doubt that he loved her. In these weeks of watching and listening and learning about her, his heart had known the truth that his mind had tried to ignore for too long.

He loved his wife.

He loved the way she laughed at terrible jokes. He loved the way she licked her lips after tasting her wine. He loved the way her eyes lit up when she saw him across a room and the way she moved so gracefully and purposely to reach him. He loved the way that she kissed him back and the way she closed her eyes and let out an exquisite sigh when he pleasured her.

No, when he made love to her.

Now that he thought back on it, they had been making love for weeks and weeks. Although she never said the words to him, he thought she returned his tender feelings. The irony struck him then, for he had fallen in love with his wife when they had so little time left to enjoy one another.

Adrian gathered her closer and she slipped her arm around his waist. The trauma of the last days was pulling him toward sleep again and he made his mind up to stay where he was.

It felt so right to be in her arms.

It felt so right to love her.

And he also decided in that moment that he would not burden her with his feelings. It was not fair to draw her in and engage her emotions when that would simply add to her pain later. He would love her quietly, with actions, not words. And when the time came and he was gone, she would remember him for the good things between them.

She would remember him....

Chapter Fourteen

"You are in love with him, aren't you?"

Miranda had tried to avoid the subject of her husband and had been successful for the whole of the morning. But now, with Lord Allendale off to his club and the children dispatched to the nursery for their afternoon naps, there was no hope of it.

"It is not a sin, Miranda. It is not as though you are confessing an *affaire de coeur* with another man." Sophie smiled and leaned closer. "He is your husband."

"I admit it, then. I love him," Miranda confessed. "I just feel that saying it aloud is somehow tempting fate."

"And his health? You were quite frightened after his attack."

"*Terrified* was more the word," she said. "Thank goodness that Lord Parker was present and knew of Windmere's condition."

Miranda stood and walked to the windows overlooking the garden. They were open and the scents of the blooming summer flowers spread through the drawing room. She inhaled deeply, enjoying them. Now that she knew of Adrian's reaction to such things, she avoided having them in the house.

"And, if I might inquire, how is his condition?"

"He has not had another attack now in four weeks. He says that Mrs. Gresham's tonics have been very helpful to him," she answered. Reaching out to touch a cascade of roses in a vase, she turned to Sophie. "And he seems to have regained his strength after being bled."

"However…" Sophie began, looking at her with an expectant expression.

"However what?"

"I can hear a very large hesitation in your answer. 'He says…' 'He seems…' As though you do not believe that all is well."

Miranda walked over and sat next to Sophie on the couch. How could she explain this without sounding like a raving lunatic or, at the least, an alarmist? "Do you remember when I noticed that something had changed in him?"

"And you went off to Windmere Park after him? Yes, I remember," Sophie replied. "That led you on to the path you walk today." She nodded, raising her eyebrows for confirmation.

"Yes. He has still not revealed the news he'd received, but he admitted that it had caused him to—to look at me…in a different light," she said, feeling the heat of a blush rising in her cheeks.

"And he rid himself of his mistress as well. A good thing to be sure." Sophie was clear on how she felt about husbands keeping women for their baser needs.

"Yes, well, I get the same kind of feeling at times. More an inkling of something wrong than anything definite. I catch him watching me and there is such sadness in his expression."

"Does he know you witness this?"

Miranda shook her head. "I think so, for when he realizes that our gazes have met, it is gone in a blink of his eyes."

Sophie took one of Miranda's hands in her own. "What do you think is the cause? Do you think it is about…there is no easy way to mention this…about your not having children yet?"

Miranda could feel the tears gather. She nodded. "It is my greatest disappointment, Sophie." She glanced at her friend's increasing girth. "He has given me so much and I cannot give him the one thing he needs to secure his titles and estates. I did not think getting in the family way was a difficult thing. After all, girls get caught all the time. My father used to mention how this one or that one married to redeem herself, and had an eight-monther." Miranda swallowed against the tears. "And look at you! You have managed three times to my none."

"Has he berated you for this?"

Miranda smiled at that. Sophie was the first to her defense. "No. We have never spoken openly about it."

"His mother, then?"

"You know that was the purpose of my visits each…" Miranda still found it uncomfortable to be too frank about these matters.

"Friday morning after a Thursday evening?"

She smiled at Sophie's straightforward manner. "Just so. Although she would never mention the issue, her disappointment in me and her disdain for my inability were apparent."

"Miranda, I am surely not the only person to recognize that no one meets the dowager's standards—of behavior, of bloodlines, of wealth. It is surprising that the old duke met her criteria for a husband."

"The kindest thing Windmere did for me was to put a stop to those visits. Now, after his mother's interference that day, I see very little of her."

"Miranda, have you never consulted anyone, a doctor or midwife, about not conceiving?"

She had thought about it many times over the last few years, but doing so seemed to her to be an admission of her barrenness. It would be putting a name to something that would then be real, and in spite of her desire to have a child, she was not yet brave enough to do that.

Miranda stood again and paced around the room, thinking on her friend's question. In truth, she would like to know if there was a reason, at least an obvious one, and there was no one other than Sophie who had spoken to her of the question. Even the dowager would never be so direct.

"Do you know of someone reputable who has some skill in this?"

"There are several physicians right here in town that specialize in womanly concerns, as well as midwives who usually handle the birthing process."

"How would I go about it, Sophie? Would Windmere need to be there?"

"I could make a few discreet inquiries for you, and set up appointments for them to come to you. Windmere's presence would be required at the physician's visit, but most likely not for a midwife's."

"So, I must speak to him about this, then?"

"If you love him and if there is a chance of discovering if there is a problem, is it not worth it?"

Miranda looked at Sophie, who at one time or another had served as friend, confidante, sister and mother figure, plus coconspirator in a number of rather daring adventures while they were in school, and smiled. Sometimes when her friend spoke with such wisdom it was difficult to remember that they were the same age.

"*If* there is a problem? We have been married for nearly seven years and I have not conceived. Surely there is a problem?"

"Ah, but you have been the Duke and Duchess of Windmere for almost five of those years," Sophie said, as though that explained it all.

"And?" Miranda clasped her hands together and sat on the couch once more.

"You could probably count the number of times he visited your bed in those years, what with the ducal responsibilities and that woman set up for his convenience. And I would be surprised if you had borne a child under those circumstances."

"Sophie! How can you be so—so…" Miranda laughed, unable to continue.

"Blunt? Why dance around it? Now that he's back in your bed, I suspect success is a short time away."

"I'd better go before you corrupt me any further, Lady Allendale. My husband still trembles in fear of another outburst from you."

"I apologized, Miranda," Sophie said as they walked to the door of the drawing room. "In writing even. And I have tried to be the very model of discretion and appropriate behavior when he is present."

"I know you are doing your best."

"I will send word as soon as I have some information for you. Then you can go forward or not."

"I want this, Sophie—for me, for Adrian and for Windmere. Forward it is."

Miranda felt better than she had in months, which was remarkable considering where she'd spent much of that time. Broaching the terribly personal topic with Sophie and hearing her suggestion would make it easier to speak to Adrian about it. Surely, he must be con-

cerned as well and would consent to any examination
necessary in pursuit of an heir.

He was reviewing some reports from one of the estates with Webb when Sherman entered.

"Your Grace? The dowager would like to call on
you, if you are receiving." The butler bowed after his an-
nouncement and waited for Adrian to reply.

"My mother is here?" Sherman had closed the study
door, so he did not know if she stood in the foyer or not.

"In her carriage, awaiting word, Your Grace."

Although a devil on his shoulder urged him to refuse
the call, Adrian would rather know her reasons for this
visit than not. He nodded at Sherman to admit her, and
then asked Webb to wait outside until he was done.

In a few minutes, his mother entered and, after a stiff
bow to each other, they both took their seats. His desk
was a sturdy enough barrier between them.

"What brings you here today, madam?"

"There is a matter that I wish to speak to you about,
Windmere."

"And that matter is…?" He would not drag this out
any longer than he had to.

"That of your worsening health and your need for
an heir."

"My health is fine, madam. Although your physician
made things worse briefly, now that I am under the care
of *qualified physicians* I am improving daily."

Her hands clenched, but he could see her fight the

urge to argue with him. It had been her own personal physician whom she had brought with her that night. In spite of knowing that Adrian would not abide being bled or being dosed to unconsciousness with laudanum, she'd ordered both.

"And the other? What progress is being made in that endeavor?"

"Madam," he said, standing to bring the interview to an end, "that is none of your business."

"As your mother and the wife of the twelfth duke, I find the continuation of our name and control of the title to be of the utmost concern."

"I repeat—" he lowered his voice and continued "—it is *none* of your concern."

"Wives have been set aside for less, Windmere. With a physician to testify to the unfortunate barren condition of the duchess, and the support of Lords and the Regent, it could be accomplished. The Warfield family must continue."

"You would endure the scandal that would surround such an action?"

"For the good of the family, I would. You have entered into too personal a relationship with Miranda and it is clouding your judgment in this. Step back and carry the title and honor as your father did, and you will see that even such a repugnant thing can work out for the best."

"Carry the title as Father did? Are you certain you want to drag up the past and admit to his mistakes, madam?"

It had taken his brother's death and five long years

of struggle to put the family back to rights. Five years of repairing the damage his father had done.

"Sherman," Adrian called out. He would probably strangle her if she did not remove herself quickly, so he strode to the door and opened it himself. The butler was a half step away and nearly fell into him. "The dowager is leaving now. Please see her to her carriage."

She nodded and left without further argument, but the damage was done. How dare she bring up the past in an effort to get rid of the one person whose arrival in the family had saved it from ruin? Only the dowager would.

He could feel the anger rising within him, but did not want, nor could he afford, another attack brought on by nervous tension. Reaching into his jacket, he took out his flask and drank directly from it, not willing to waste time on finding a glass. Mrs. Gresham had been contacted and had sent new instructions and new ingredients for the dispensation of the elixir she suggested. This new one burned his throat, but seemed to work faster and more thoroughly than the last one had.

He sat in his chair, leaned his head back and breathed in a slow, even manner. Or as slowly and evenly as he could manage now that he was outraged by his mother's suggestion. Thinking of her incredible gall, he shook his head.

Even if such a suggestion was considered, and he would not, there would not be enough time to go through the arduous process of ending the marriage. It would take well over a year in the church and courts, and Parliament's speed of handling something like this would be anyone's guess. Beyond that, it was simply not done. And that his mother, with her standards of behavior, would come up with such a suggestion was frightening.

Did she know the truth of his health? Was she gambling that he could outlive the length of time needed to rid himself of one wife and get another? The duke he'd been even up until a few months ago would have jumped at her offer.

Now he was a man in love with his wife who wanted her protection first. A son could be raised to take over control of the estates and continue the nurturing and growth that he'd contributed since taking over at his brother's death. A son could enlarge and expand the industries Adrian was investing in for the future of the family. A son…

Well, he'd certainly been doing his part to beget one, and Miranda had entered into it with an acceptance and joy that made it no chore. It was one of the best parts of falling in love with one's wife, he realized. The other would be to hear her tell him that she loved him.

Shifting in the chair, he immediately thought differently. No, he was convinced that his course of action was the correct one. Continue his efforts to give her a child, and if that did not work in time, ensure her future by making arrangements for a house and an income that would provide a safe place for her to live. And, of course, his newest plan—find Miranda's next husband.

Parker had balked, but had come up with a list of potential candidates for consideration. Adrian had done the same, and now that list sat on his desk. They'd removed any wastrels, rakes or drunkards. Also, any youngish man of noble birth who needed an heir was eliminated from consideration, since no guarantee could be given about that situation. Adrian was left with a list of men whom he thought would be suitable for her in their natures, manners and livings.

Now, as he reached over and pulled open the portfolio revealing the names, he was saddened by the need for it. Closing his eyes for a moment, he prayed for things to be different. To be given the chance to be with her and to grow old with her.

Suddenly, as if she'd been conjured from his thoughts, she stood before him.

"Miranda," he said, beginning to stand.

"No, please." She waved him back to his chair. "I did not mean to disturb you. Webb told me you were in here alone and I thought we might talk. If you have a moment, of course."

In spite of the lightness in her voice, there were shadows in her eyes. Something was bothering her. Everything about the way she held herself, rigid and aloof, warned him. Had she discovered the truth about him?

He stood and walked to her side. "Is there something wrong?" Taking her hand in his, he kissed it and held it as he guided her to a chair.

"I would prefer to stand, if you do not mind."

Adrian backed away and leaned against his desk. What

could have her so serious? He watched as she did what he usually did when pondering a problem—paced the room. She removed her bonnet and dropped it on a table as she passed, but still she would not look at him directly.

"Miranda," he said softly. "What is it?"

"I understand the dowager was here earlier."

"Yes, she was. Does this concern her?" Had his mother approached Miranda with the same suggestion?

"In a way," she said. Finally she faced him and then sat in the chair nearest him. "This actually concerns all of us, but most especially you, Adrian." He watched as she twisted her hands together, and his stomach twisted as well.

"How so?"

"I know that your mother and brother only permitted our marriage because of the settlement made by my father."

"I had some say in it, too, Miranda," he said.

"I know you did, but if the dowry I brought had not been adequate, even generous, and if the agreement did not allow that most of it could be used for the upkeep of the Warfield estates, the dowager would never have considered me. Truly, Adrian, I have always known this and am not insulted by it. It is the way of things."

"What brought this up, Miranda? The estates, thanks to the influx of that money, now thrive. Our tenants are well, the lands produce well and the family's interests flourish."

"But the family does not."

"The *family…?*" The realization hit him. "You speak of us not having children yet." So, she was worried as well?

"Yes, Adrian. As much as you have been patient about it, my failure in this is apparent. Even in spite of our more recent increased frequency of…marital…congress, I have failed to conceive."

"I do not blame you, Miranda." *I love you,* he thought. The rest would work out if they had more time, he was certain.

"I had a very frank discussion about this today with Sophie…."

"Lady Allendale? You discussed our procreation or lack of it with that woman?"

"I know you two rub each other the wrong way, but she is my closest and dearest friend. Who else would I talk with about things of this nature?"

"Who indeed?" he replied, wanting to be angry. But he knew he had shared some personal information with Parker. "And Lady Allendale's recommendations?"

"Do not sound offended, please. We spoke in only the broadest of terms."

"I am not angry, Miranda. I just was not aware that this was a concern you had."

"We both know the purpose of marriage, Adrian, and we also know that ours has not been successful in that area. Sophie simply suggested that I should consult, discreetly of course, with a reputable physician who treats these types of problems to see if one exists."

"A physician, eh?" He hesitated to endorse such an

idea due to his own rather varied experience with doctors lately.

"And a midwife as well. She suggested the one who has attended her in the past and who will be at this birth also."

He gave a start, not having realized Miranda's friend was increasing. "I did not know about that."

"It is not public news yet."

She was in pain; he could see it in her eyes as she thought about her friend's news. He walked to her and opened his arms. She stepped into them and accepted his embrace and the comfort he tried to offer her. She did not begin to cry as he thought she might.

"I am happy for them, Adrian, and I want us to share the same kind of joy. I believe that Sophie's suggestion is a good one, and I would rather know the truth than live under some pretense. You can understand that, can you not?"

Her words tore through him. She was decrying his present behavior without even knowing it, and he felt guilty that he had not shared his truth with her. But it was still better for her not to know the type of news he would tell her.

"I can." He held her away and then kissed her. "If this is what you want to do, I give my permission for these consultations. Please tell me when you schedule them and I will be there."

"I will. Now, I should let you get back to your work." She picked up her bonnet and gloves from the table and walked toward the door.

He could not let her escape without kissing her and making her know how he felt about her. He was at her side before she could touch the doorknob, and had his arms around her, pulling her closer. Touching his lips to her mouth, he breathed in her sweetness and tasted her acceptance. His precious Miranda offered all that she had to him.

"Miranda," he whispered.

She looked into his eyes and saw so much emotion there. Another man might have blamed her. Another man might have treated her with disdain and continued to humiliate her with other women. All she could see in his eyes was his concern and caring. Overwhelmed by it, she kissed him and then pulled away.

"I…"

I love you, Adrian, she almost said aloud. She'd said it so many times in her mind since she'd discovered it to be true. "I wondered what the dowager wanted here, if I might ask?"

Had he heard the hitch in her voice? She did not want to burden him by sharing the feelings within her when it was not what he wanted from a wife. Oh, their situation was definitely different than before, but it was still marriage. They cared about each other and were more affectionate to each other, even outside of their chambers. They spent more time together and spoke more to one another. With his health concerns, and now that the subject of an heir had been broached between them, this was not the time to add the matter of soft feelings to the discussion.

"The dowager?" he asked, looking around the room. "Oh, my mother was here about…something about the…she asked my opinion about some possible suitors for Miss Stevenson." Adrian looked over at the desk, and Miranda noticed a list of names on top of his other papers.

"Is it something I could help you with? I would certainly be willing to give my insight into any whom I have met or know."

Adrian paused for a moment and then the strangest of smiles crossed his face—one filled with poignancy and humor. "Actually, it could be an immense help to me if you would. A woman's insight would be just the thing in convincing Miss Stevenson, if the need arises."

He moved behind his desk and took up a quill. "If you might mention anything you know about these men that might be objectionable? Not so much the positives as any known negatives to them being considered good matches."

"I think I can manage that." She smiled, glad that the focus of their conversation had changed from the profound to something more practical.

"Sir Thomas Brown, lately of Devonshire."

"He is a barrister?"

"Yes, and recently knighted for services to the Crown."

"No objections."

"Baron Lindsay?"

"I did not know he was looking for a wife," she said.

"Recently out of mourning." He scribbled a note on the paper and then read out another to her. "Baron William Parker, heir to Viscount Parker."

"Lord Parker? Our Lord Parker?" Shaking her head, she laughed. "That did not come out as I meant it to."

Adrian's gaze became intense. "What did you mean to say?"

"I thought that he was a given in this. The dowager has invited him to several suppers and he has paid calls on Miss Stevenson. I thought she would have asked your opinion of a match between them long ago."

"She did ask me. I am asking for your opinion on it now."

"I think it would be a fine match. They are of a similar nature and their ages are not so far apart. He seems to enjoy her company in spite of the good-hearted teasing he does. He is respectful of her. A good match would be possible between them."

Adrian stared at Miranda for a moment before looking back at his list. There was some tension underlying this process. Perhaps he felt put upon by his mother to take part in it when Miss Stevenson was not even family?

"Do you see some problem in that match? He is your friend, after all. You would know him better than I would."

"I would have no objection to a match," he said quietly.

They spent another quarter hour reviewing names, recommending some and objecting to others, until she realized something about the list.

"I just noticed something about all of these men, save Lord Parker."

"What is that?"

"In addition to them being married previously, there is a marked difference in age between all these men and Miss Stevenson."

Adrian frowned and looked at the names. "Married before? Ah, just so. As to their ages, most hover near the age of forty, not much older than I am. Is that too ancient?"

"For an older matron like myself, no. But Miss Stevenson is still at a tender age and the difference may be too great."

"An older matron? Is that how you see yourself?"

"I am just past a score and seven, much closer to your age and theirs than Miss Stevenson is at but ten and eight."

He smiled at her and she grew warm under his gaze. "Now I see your meaning. She is quite young."

"This is her first Season, as well. It is possible that she will wait for another before settling down."

Miranda's husband frowned again as though he had not thought of this possibility. Then he nodded. "Well, I will note your concern over their ages."

"You are too kind," she said sarcastically, causing him to laugh aloud.

"Are you free now or do you have some engagement to run off to?" He dabbed the quill to clean it ard then put it back in the tray. Stuffing the papers back in his portfolio, he looked at her with a barely suppressed smile threatening the edges of his mouth.

"I have nothing until the ball this evening at Lord and Lady Harbridge's." She wrapped her gloves around her fingers.

"Then, if you would be so kind as to accompany me upstairs, I would like to show you something that might appeal to older matrons such as yourself."

Adrian walked around the desk and held out his hand to her. Miranda saw this as the sham it was, but whenever he got that mischievous glint in his eyes, it foretold of a wonderful afternoon for her.

"Truly?" She took his hand and walked with him up the stairs to his chambers.

"All this talk of marriage makes me eager to claim my wife."

"And, Your Grace," she whispered as they passed by servants busy polishing the railings, "will this be behavior appropriate or inappropriate to someone of your standing?" She could feel her body preparing itself already for his touch. She began to breathe faster as they approached his door.

"Completely inappropriate, I fear. And something never dared with someone of a tender age. Only an older matron would survive it," he teased.

The heat grew and she felt droplets of perspiration bead up and trickle down her back. She needed to set aside the terribly serious worries of their discussions for a while, and this would be the perfect distraction.

Some hours later, after a light meal to refresh themselves, they climbed into the ducal carriage and went off to the Earl of Harbridge's ball. Miranda realized as Adrian sat next to her with his hand possessively and inappropriately on her thigh, that she did feel claimed.

And loved from head to toe and every inch in between.

Chapter Fifteen

"You seem nervous."

"I am nervous."

"Try to calm yourself. It cannot be a good thing to be nervous when you are examined. Lady Allendale will be present during the interview with the midwife and I will be with you when the physician is here."

Adrian stood behind her at the dressing table as she brushed her hair. She hoped that the trembling in her hands was not as apparent as it felt to her. This morning's appointments were crucial to their lives, and she both wanted and feared the outcome.

"What if…?" She began, but could not finish the obvious question on her mind.

Adrian crouched down behind her so that their eyes met in the looking glass. Wrapping his arms around her, he squeezed her.

"You are the brave one, Miranda. As you said, it is

better to know if there is a problem than to live with this fear and ignorance."

"I do confess that I am not feeling very brave at this moment." Why had she pressed for this? If he had not raised the question of her fertility or lack of it, why had she?

Because something had changed between them months ago that was a catalyst for so many other things. And although he had referred to it, he had never revealed what the incident was that had sparked all the rest.

"This is something that we should have attended to sooner. Now we will find the answer we seek," he said.

"Why did we not, Adrian? Why is it such an issue now and not before?" Each time she looked back at the series of events that had brought them to this moment of both bliss and terror, it all pointed back to that day in the spring when he'd got drunk. "What changed those months ago to make this so important now?"

He paled at her words and released her, standing behind her, then walking a few steps away.

"Something happened to you. Tell me that I might understand."

He offered her a weak smile and shook his head. "As I told you before, there is nothing that you need worry about."

"Adrian, I want to know…" she said, stopping when a knock sounded at the door.

"When it is time, we will talk about it," he said as he pulled the door open.

"Your Grace, Lady Allendale is here. She asked to

meet you in the drawing room." Fisk looked at Adrian and he nodded.

"Finish dressing and come down." He kissed Miranda's cheek and walked past Fisk. "See to Her Grace now."

He felt guilty putting her off, but he was not prepared nor willing to reveal it all to her yet. It simply was not the time. As he left the room to meet with the midwife brought by Lady Allendale, he wondered if he ever would declare it to be such a time.

Whatever preconceived notions he had about the woman Lady Allendale was bringing to discuss the duchess's concern, the one who curtsied before him did not fit them. Instead of a middle-aged or older woman, this one seemed too young to be experienced in the science of midwifery. Apparently he spoke the words aloud, for both Lady Allendale and the woman stared at him.

"Forgive me, Mrs.…?"

"Mrs. James, Your Grace. Mrs. Mark James," she said as she rose and stood before him.

"Mrs. James, thank you for coming. I believe that Lady Allendale has explained the cause for this call and our need for discretion."

Lady Allendale sighed loudly and then glared at him. "Mrs. James can be relied upon for her abilities and her discretion, Your Grace."

Offering them both a seat and waiting for them to take it, he also offered refreshments, which were declined.

"I suspect that you would like to know exactly what

my abilities are," Mrs. James said, smiling at him. "I believe my age has made you somewhat doubtful that I can be involved in the practice of midwifery."

He nodded and listened as she explained her background, and realized that he respected her not only for what she had done, but also what she planned to do. As the daughter of a battleground surgeon and then as the wife of a soldier, Mrs. James had found herself treating all types of injuries as one of very few women with any medical knowledge in the camps that grew up around the battlegrounds of France.

Gradually she began to care for the women during childbirth. After her husband had been killed, she remained there, working as she had, until returning to her family several years ago. Now, combining her experience and the additional training she'd sought at various hospitals and colleges, she practiced midwifery.

"Although I claim some experience at helping women through childbirth, I cannot in all good conscience claim an expertise in why some women do not conceive, Your Grace."

"I certainly appreciate your candor, Mrs. James. Tell me why you are here then, if not to help with this problem."

"Lady Allendale has given her permission for me to reveal certain personal facts about her to you. If I may?"

Lady Allendale nodded and then looked away as though disinterested. Adrian nodded for her to continue.

"Lady Allendale has a particular difficulty in giving birth, which I discovered during her first birth and was able to assist with during her second. I have a knowledge of female anatomy that helped determine the cause of her trouble and, so far, we've been able to deliver her children safely."

This was more information of a personal nature or any other than Adrian wanted to know about Lady Allendale. His cravat felt entirely too high, too starched and too tight right now, and he tugged at the edge of it to relieve the pressure.

"Your Grace, we felt it important for you to know the extent of my abilities. I did not mean to speak with such frankness if it offends you."

"I am not offended, Mrs. James. Indeed, I find a new respect for your work due to your words. And how can this help the duchess?"

"I will examine her to determine if there are any abnormalities in her structure that would seem to prevent her from carrying a baby to term."

This was entirely too much for any male, even one exposing himself to this type of conversation for all the right reasons. He'd had enough. Lucky for him, Miranda arrived just then and he stood, planning to make an escape.

"I will leave you to your business and be in my study if you need me," he said, nodding to them as he passed Miranda at the door.

"Your Grace? May I have a moment of your time before you leave?" Mrs. James greeted the duchess and then followed him into the hall.

"Is he blushing, Sophie?" Miranda asked as her husband and Mrs. James spoke in the hall.

"I believe he is," Sophie said, looking past her. "I must admit he held up longer than I thought he would." She laughed as Miranda sat down next to her on the couch. "And when Mrs. James mentioned my problem, I thought he turned a bit green."

Mrs. James returned and explained the process to both of them. When Miranda would have felt some embarrassment, Mrs. James's calm manner helped her through it. In a half hour's time and after lots of questions and some not uncomfortable poking, prodding and pressing, it was over, and Mrs. James asked that the duke be summoned.

Although she had been at Miranda's side through it all, Sophie excused herself when Adrian entered the room. Fisk waited at the door and took Lady Allendale off to freshen herself while the couple spoke in private with Mrs. James.

Although Miranda thought he would stand while receiving this report, Adrian surprised her by sitting at her side. When he took her hand in his and squeezed it, not letting it go, she felt her heart lighten. No matter the news, he was there.

"Your Grace, I found nothing abnormal in my examination of the duchess. I could feel no blockages or unusual growths that would seem to prevent conception or pregnancy."

"Is there anything else?"

"From the answers you both gave, I suspect there is nothing wrong."

"Then why have I not conceived?" Miranda asked.

"It takes some women longer than others, Your Grace."

"We have been married for seven years. Surely that is time enough to accomplish such a thing?" Her frustration was coming through in her voice. Even she could hear it.

"I'm afraid that is not something I can answer. But I think that the news is good. I cannot find any problem physically to cause this."

"So there is hope, then?" Adrian asked, squeezing her hand once more.

"I do believe there is. With time and a certain level of attention to this…" Mrs. James paused and smiled at both of them. Miranda knew exactly what the woman meant. "…I think you will have children." The midwife stood and curtsied. "I think this has been a rather exhausting appointment for you both, so I will go now."

"My thanks, Mrs. James. For your help and advice," Miranda exclaimed.

"It has been my honor, Your Grace. Your secretary has my directions if you need me for anything. Please do not hesitate to call."

Sherman opened the door and showed Mrs. James out. Sophie returned a moment later.

"I will not ask what she said, but was she helpful to you?"

"She was, Sophie. I thank you for suggesting her," Miranda replied.

"I am grateful, too, Lady Allendale."

Miranda could tell it was difficult for Adrian to say the words. Sophie looked as though she might tease him over it, but then thought better of it and just nodded.

"I am due at home and, since you do not need me for the next appointment, I will take my leave."

"Allow me to walk you to the door," Adrian added, following her friend out into the hallway.

Miranda could see them exchanging words. Then Sophie looked at the duke in shock, and he dipped his head and nodded to her.

Miranda was not certain what had happened, so she waited for his return. "What did you say to her? I have never seen quite that expression on her face before."

"I may live to regret this, but I told her she was welcome here at any time."

"Did you? I know how difficult it was for you to make such an offer."

His face showed a mix of regret, horror and resignation. She laughed for a moment and then quieted as she realized they had to talk about Mrs. James's visit. Miranda sat back down and watched as Adrian poured himself a glass of brandy. Although she could use something to help her calm her nerves and fortify herself for Dr. Blake's call, she did not dare ask for a dose. The thought of the same examination being conducted by a man, even with her husband at her side, was somewhat overwhelming.

"Overall, Mrs. James was more hopeful than I thought she would be," Adrian began. "Did you think her credible?"

"You spoke to her at some length before I arrived. Did she speak to you about her experience and training?"

"Miranda, you have just answered my question with a question of your own." He sat down at her side again and took her hand. "Tell me what *you* thought of her."

"Sophie has such confidence in her. Now, after meeting her and talking to her myself, I do as well."

"I was quite impressed by her manner of investigating and her knowledge. And, of course, she told us what we wanted to hear." A frown settled on his brow as he looked at Miranda. "Still, I think she is correct in this. There is nothing wrong that enough time and attention will not resolve."

He took another mouthful of brandy and Miranda knew that if he met her gaze, she would see that sad, almost mournful expression there. What could she do for him now?

"I do not mind the attention, Adrian."

He did smile then and raised his glass in a salute. "Nor do I." He glanced across the room at the clock on the mantel. "What time do we expect Dr. Blake to arrive?"

"In about an hour or so."

"Would you excuse me for a short time? I have some papers to look over." He stood, but didn't wait for her reply. "I will return before Dr. Blake arrives."

Miranda watched him leave, knowing something was

profoundly wrong. Instead of the joy or, at the least, relief over the midwife's comments, he appeared to be bothered by them. Certainly Mrs. James had outlined her limitations, but overall, Miranda felt a sense of hope at her prognosis. She supposed that her husband was being more pragmatic over it.

She rang for tea, and asked for the strong coffee that he so liked to be delivered to Adrian in his study, while they waited for the "preeminent Dr. Blake," as Sophie had described him. Her friend had no personal knowledge of him, but had been referred to him by several others. And, of course, he had attended several of the queen's children's births. Miranda had even secured a copy of his treatise on childbirth and his opinions of the "expected behavior of women of good character during their lying-in."

Not that she was near to that "revered and anticipated" state, but she found the presentation to be lacking in firm details about the process itself. If the doctor was anything like his writing style, it would be an interesting meeting.

Miranda had just finished her tea when Adrian returned. "I heard the carriage outside. He is here."

There was a commotion in the hallway as he entered, and then Sherman announced him and opened the door to the drawing room, wider and wider, until it could go no farther. Dr. Blake was the largest man she'd ever beheld. He turned to the side to enter the room and then faced them.

"Your Grace." He nodded to Adrian and then to her. "Madam."

"Dr. Blake, thank you for coming," Adrian said.

"I do not commonly visit patients or prospective patients." He glanced at Miranda and then back to him. "I came as a favor to your mother, the dowager," he replied. "I have known her for many years."

Adrian nearly stopped the interview at that moment. He could see Miranda tense at the mention of his mother, as well. Before he could do anything, the doctor continued, "Now, what seems to be the problem?" Dr. Blake looked around the room, most likely for a place to sit, but there was none save the couch that would hold his bulky figure.

"Your Grace?" Sherman asked from the doorway. At Adrian's nod, two of the footman came in carrying a large bench.

"Very good, Sherman," he said, smiling at his butler's ingenuity and quick thinking. They placed it in the middle of the open spot opposite the couch and left.

The doctor quickly settled on it, pulled out a notebook and opened it. Then, with a snap, he closed it, stored it back in his pocket and looked at him.

"Just a few questions of the duchess before we continue."

Miranda nodded. This had such a different tone than the earlier appointment, and Adrian wondered how she would handle its demands.

"Your mother is alive?"

"No, she died when I was three."

"Childbirth, then?"

Miranda paused and shook her head. "Consumption."

"Are you her only child?"

"Yes, I was born a year after her marriage, and then she became ill."

"Consumption related to reproduction is not uncommon at all." He frowned and looked at Miranda. "How old were you when your cycles began?"

Adrian shifted uncomfortably. The doctor's manner offered no reassurance or softness in his tone or questions, and his process seemed to have none of the structure and logic that Mrs. James had used in hers. But Miranda answered.

"I was fifteen years old."

"Your most recent one ended when?"

Although she blinked in surprise, she answered, "Three weeks ago."

"Dr. Blake," Adrian interrupted.

"Well, thank you, Your Grace," Dr. Blake said, rising and nodding to Miranda. "That will be all."

Finding the doctor's actions brusque almost to the point of rudeness, Adrian stood in turn. "Dr. Blake, I do not think that—"

Interrupting again, the doctor nodded to Miranda. "Let us allow the duchess to retire and we will discuss this matter." A barely noticeable bow accompanied the order.

Now it was Adrian's turn to be astonished. Or not. He'd found before that physicians tended to ignore the patient involved when discussing their diagnoses or plans. The fact that Blake would discuss it with the patient's husband should be no surprise.

"Allow me to meet with the doctor, my dear." Adrian held out his hand to her and escorted her to the door. She was shaking, but Adrian was positive that was not due to nervousness but anger. "I will call you when he is gone."

She left without a word and he turned to find the doctor already seated. Apparently renowned physicians needed no good manners in their repertoire of behavior. Adrian walked to the sideboard and poured himself a glass of brandy.

"I find that women are such emotional creatures it is far better to continue such discussions without their presence. Their delicate natures cannot tolerate such things."

Blake could not have been speaking about Miranda. Yes, she was emotional, but she was courageous and bold and steely when she needed to be. Hell, Adrian had no doubt that he was alive because of her ability to take control when she needed to. He cleared his throat and brought his attention back to the doctor.

"When did you marry, Your Grace?"

"The duchess and I have been married for just over seven years." Adrian waited for the next question.

"And you conduct marital relations?"

"Yes." He swallowed another mouthful of brandy.

"Have you any injuries of a certain nature that would preclude you from producing children?"

"None. Although I do have allergic—"

Dr. Blake raised a hand to stop him from saying any more. With great effort, the man stood. "The duchess, I fear, is barren."

"Barren? On what do you base that diagnosis?"

"Her history is perfectly clear in this matter—her mother died of reproductive consumption, the duchess was abnormally late in coming into womanhood and seven years without conception."

Miranda had not said her mother's death was related to her giving birth. And was fifteen truly too old? Did that indicate a problem? "But, Doctor—" Adrian began.

With a hand in the air, Dr. Blake stopped him once more. "I know that this is difficult news to accept, Your Grace. However, it is my professional opinion that she will never bear children. I will leave it to you, as her husband, to convey this unfortunate news to her. If I can be of service to you on any other matter, please contact me at once."

Adrian could not believe the speed with which the man could vacate a room. He offered his pronouncement and then was gone.

Sherman came to close the door and asked if His Grace had need of anything. Shaking his head, Adrian walked to the window and stared out.

Still reeling over the doctor's manner and his words, he wondered where the truth lay for him and Miranda. If the midwife was to be believed, they needed only time to solve the problem, and that was something he did not have. If the physician was correct, time would not matter. Either way was a hopeless one for him.

"That bad?" she asked from behind him. "I tried to be the good wife and wait for your call, but the anticipation was too great."

He turned and pulled her into his arms, needing to feel her there, against his heart. They stood quietly for some minutes before he lifted his head and kissed her forehead.

"You are a good wife, Miranda, never doubt that," he whispered.

"I was surprised to have their differences be so marked, Adrian. And I confess that I am relieved Dr. Blake did not examine me." She stepped away and sat on the couch, sliding to one side to make room for Adrian. "Sit and tell me, although I suspect I already know."

"He believes that you are…" He could not say the word. Even if he made himself not think it true, the word was so powerful.

"Barren," she said. "I expected that." Her voice was filled with sadness. "And do you think he is correct?"

"I would like to believe that Mrs. James's assessment is the correct one," he said, even though it offered him only slightly more hope than the doctor's. Of course, if he was successful in his efforts to set up a new life for her, Miranda might yet have the joy of a child with her next husband.

That hurt, though he wanted her to be happy, the possibility that she would be that way with someone else was terribly difficult to accept.

"And we have no way of knowing who is right." She leaned against him. "I had hoped for more than this."

"Well, Miranda, let us look at this logically, although the good doctor doubts in a woman's ability to do so." He smiled, and she smiled back. "If Dr. Blake is right, there is nothing to be done. If Mrs. James is correct, we need do nothing that we are not already doing."

They spent a time just sitting together, each lost in their own thoughts, hopes and dreams. Why did all the important things not matter until they were lost to you? Why had he not taken advantage of the years they'd had together? So much time gone and there was no telling how much might be left to them.

That night, when he took her into his bed, he loved her as though it was their last time together on this earth. With a despair he'd not felt before, he searched for that elusive place in her arms and emptied himself into her willing heart and womb. The prayer, one of a man desperately in love with his wife, and one whose time was running out, was the same.

For Miranda.

For Miranda.

Chapter Sixteen

"**S**ir Thomas, it is so nice to you again. Lady Marsh has quite the crush here tonight!" Miranda offered her hand to the barrister as he stepped closer after Adrian presented him.

"It is that, Your Grace. At least the weather has given us a bit of a cooling off."

Sir Thomas Brown, recently knighted by the Regent for services to the Crown, was a tall man, nearing forty. His eyes twinkled in the light of hundreds of candles and he smiled at something Adrian said. Miranda tried to listen, but the noise of those around her made it difficult. She leaned closer.

"Are you staying in town for the rest of Season?" she asked.

"Yes, Your Grace. This is my daughter's first one and I am trying to muddle through it."

She now remembered two more things about him—

she'd met his daughter, a delightful young woman, at an afternoon musicale that she'd attended with Miss Stevenson, and he'd recently completed the expected mourning for the death of his wife.

"Your daughter—Cassandra, is it not?—has such a talent on the flute. And it must be so difficult handling this on your own," she murmured, touching his arm. "Sir Thomas, you have my condolences."

"Thank you, ma'am," he said, nodding in acceptance.

Just as she was about to draw Adrian back into the conversation, the majordomo announced dinner, and it was time to eat.

"My dear, I see someone who has just arrived that I need to speak with. Sir Thomas, would you be so kind as to escort Her Grace into dinner?" Adrian peered over the crowd toward the doors leading to the entryway.

"It would be my honor, Your Grace." Sir Thomas bowed and offered his arm.

"Windmere? Are you certain?" she asked.

He kissed her hand and smiled. "I apologize for this, but I really must go. My thanks, Sir Thomas, for stepping into the breach for me."

He disappeared into the crowd, which moved toward several adjoining rooms set with a number of small tables, rather than one very large, formal dining area. It made things more casual, Miranda decided, as, after filling their plates at the extensive buffet, they were led by the butler to a table.

Her initial concern when she saw that they were

seated alone vanished as Sir Thomas entertained her with stories of his home in Devonshire and as they commiserated over the experiences of chaperoning young women through the social chaos known as the Season. Although she looked for Adrian, he did not return to the dining rooms nor to the ball.

When Sir Thomas asked her to dance, she did, all the while watching for her husband. Quite a pleasant man, and a gentleman, he walked with her until they located Lady Allendale and released her into her friend's company. For the fourth time in two weeks, Adrian had gone off without her.

Parker came back into the small parlor and closed the door behind him.

"Lock it, if you please," Adrian said.

"Done," his friend said. Sitting down across the table from him, he nodded. "And done."

"They were talking?"

"Yes. And things seemed very friendly between them."

"And the table?"

Parker scowled at this question. "I made certain that the butler seated them at the smallest table for two, as you directed." He stood and walked over to the paintings hanging on one wall. "I cannot say I like this, Windmere. Is it truly necessary?"

"As I told you, I want to see which of them she favors."

"I still think you should simply tell her the truth about this…about you. You told me how Dr. Blake's attitude angered you, and now you are treating her in the same manner, making this decision for her."

Adrian shook his head. "I do not think it is time."

"Not time? I will be telling the tearful widow over your coffin by the time you decide it is time!" Parker turned and glared at him. "She is your greatest hope and your greatest help, Adrian. Give her the truth and let her be on your side for this. Who knows what can happen?"

"I know what will happen," he said, gritting his teeth. "She will suffer the pain of knowing. I do not fool myself into believing that she loves me, but I know she will feel some loss at my death."

Parker stared at him unmoving for a moment and then burst out laughing. He laughed so hard that it caused him to double over at the waist. And still he laughed. A few minutes later, he wiped at his eyes and pointed at Adrian.

"You are as blind as a stump, my friend, if you think she does not love you."

"I do not want her to love me," he countered. "It…it is not fair…" He stopped, unable to explain all the things that rampaged through his mind and his heart when he thought of the short time they had left.

"She loves you, Adrian, as you love her. Any fool can see it when you look at each other or talk together. Now tell her," he said, walking over to stand in front of him, "so that every precious moment you have left to you is not wasted. Do not lose this time." Will held out his hand and Adrian took it, shaking it.

"When did you become such a philosopher?" he asked, surprised at the depth of understanding from a man not yet acquainted with the married state.

"Apparently while attending the endless discussions of classic literature and history and philosophy that Miss Stevenson seems to find so interesting."

"Oh? So that is the way of it, then?" He smiled at something that had been foregone in his own mind for many weeks. "Is there an offer in the works? Or does she not return your tender feelings?"

Parker looked as though he would throw a punch at him, but scowled instead. "She and I have an understanding, Adrian. We have spoken of it and Juliet, Miss Stevenson, wishes to enjoy the rest of the Season before making any announcements."

"And does my mother know yet?"

"Um…no."

"Wise of you both. Make your plans, then inform the dowager."

"Listen to me," Will said, lowering his voice. "Talk to the duchess. Tell her the truth. Live this time you have together to the fullest."

"I will think on it."

"Adrian, please?"

"I will think on it."

He could tell that Parker wanted to continue the argument, but his friend stepped down and, with a quiet farewell, went off to see if it was time for his dance with Miss Stevenson.

Adrian followed a few minutes later. He stood near the top of the steps leading out of the ballroom and watched Miranda dance with Sir Thomas. She wore her hair piled on top of her head, with a few long curls following the contours of her neck. The gown, cut fashionably low and exposing far too much of the slopes of her bosom, set off her complexion and eyes to perfection. When she laughed at something Sir Thomas said while they made their way through the steps of the dance, Adrian's heart seemed to stutter.

As the dance came to an end and he observed her laughing and enjoying herself, he knew he could not approach her now. Not until he'd made a decision about how they would live the next few months, the last few months of his life, if the doctors were correct.

Adrian found his way out and took his carriage to his club. After several hours of mindless card games and chatter with friends, he went home, still unsure about disclosing the truth to her. But when he stood at the end of her bed, watching her sleep, he knew what he had to do.

"I am telling you, Sophie. It is the strangest thing and it is true."

"Come now, Miranda. Why would he do something like that?"

Miranda leaned nearer the window and watched the carriages roll down the street. Peering past the drapes, she tapped her foot, trying to make sense of it. "I do not understand it, but I assure you that I know when I am being foisted on someone else."

"Foisted? Oh, Miranda!" Sophie said, laughing now. "I have this image in my mind now of you being handed bodily from one gentleman to another. Picture the quadrille, where instead of moving through the steps, the gentlemen pass you down the rows, one end to the other!"

Miranda could not help but smile now that she could imagine the same scene in her mind. "Making light of this is not answering my concerns."

"Sit down and let us try to reason through it, then."

She turned away from the window and nodded. Sitting across from Sophie, she thought about the chain of events that had her so confused.

"When was the first time you think this happened?"

"About three—no, four weeks ago."

"And Windmere left you in the company of another man?"

"No, it is more than that, Sophie. He retrieved the gentleman, brought him to me, made certain we were acquainted and chatting, and then left on some pretext or another of being needed elsewhere."

"Oh, la! Now I can see Windmere like a hunting dog, sniffing out his quarry, dragging them to you and dropping them at your feet."

"I did not recognize your quaint sense of humor before, Sophie," she said a bit sharply. "I am sorry, but you do not seem to be taking this with as much seriousness as I'd hoped."

"Miranda, I do apologize. I did not get much rest last night and it feels as though the most random things occur to me when I am tired."

She reached over and touched Sophie's hand. "Are you unwell? Is it the…your condition?"

"I believe it is related. I have the strangest urgings and cravings at this point in the pregnancy. Last time, it was strawberry jam. I wanted strawberry jam at the oddest hours and on the strangest foods. I drove Cook mad trying to keep enough on hand to meet my requirements. I swore the baby would be born holding a scone smothered in jam."

"That would have been a sight to see, Sophie. But I am certain that Mrs. James would handle it without hesitation."

Lord Allendale walked by the open door of the drawing room at that moment and paused to look in.

"Your Grace," he said, nodding to her. "My dear," he said to Sophie, gifting his wife with a very wicked smile. He left as quickly as he'd arrived, and Miranda turned back to her friend.

"And this time? What do you crave this time?"

"Not what," Sophie whispered. Looking around, she leaned over and continued, "Whom."

"Whom? Whom do you crave?" Miranda said the words before she realized the meaning. "Oh, Sophie!" she exclaimed as she now recognized the smile on Lord Allendale's face. She could feel her own face blushing with heat. She laughed. "Hence the lack of rest?"

"Just so." Sophie reached up and tucked a loose lock of hair back into the pin holding it, and smiled. "And it is so much more enjoyable than strawberry jam."

Unable to believe that Sophie had revealed such a thing to her, Miranda laughed again. "Can we discuss my problem now or should I allow you to find your husband?"

"I will try to focus." She took a breath and let it out slowly. "There now, tell me again how many times this has happened?"

"Six. At two balls, one afternoon musicale, two dinners and once in our box at the theater."

Sophie frowned. "And gentlemen all?"

"Two knights of the Empire, two barons and twice with the same earl. Peers and gentlemen."

"This is peculiar," she said. "And you had made the acquaintance of all of these men before this happened?"

"Yes. At some point in the last month, Windmere introduced them to me or had them introduced to me."

"Very strange indeed."

"The strangest part is that they were all on the list of men that the dowager asked Windmere to review as potential matches for Miss Stevenson."

Sophie stood and walked to the tray on the sideboard. She might not be craving strawberry jam, but she did seem hungry much more often than usual. Picking out a few pieces of sliced cake and fruit, she offered some to Miranda.

"Another regrettable consequence of breeding, Miranda. Constant hunger...for food." She came back and sat down. "Do you think that might be the reason? Perhaps he is looking for your opinion before considering their offers for Miss Stevenson?"

"No, that cannot be it. All one has to do is watch Lord Parker and Miss Stevenson at the same event to know where the true offer will come from."

"You said his name was on the dowager's list?"

"He was. And he is usually somewhere close by when Windmere leaves. Most of the times when it has happened, he is the one who calls Windmere aside."

"So he is involved in this somehow?" Sophie asked.

"I believe so, or at least his actions would seem to implicate him."

"This is indeed very strange."

Miranda felt thirsty now so she helped herself to some tea. She knew what she needed to do; she was simply looking for Sophie's concurrence on her course of action. Her patience for Adrian's avoidance was at an end. Their relationship had come so very far from where it was back in the spring that she would not allow this situation to continue.

"You know what you must do, do you not, Miranda?" Sophie asked quietly.

"Yes."

"I am here as your friend. You know that."

"I do, Sophie. You cannot know how much I appreciate having you as a friend."

Miranda finished her tea and smoothed her gown over her lap. "Now?"

"I see no reason to delay further."

"Absolutely."

Both women rose to their feet. But before she let her go, Sophie threw her arms around Miranda and hugged her tightly.

There was nothing else for them to say, and Miranda wanted to return home as quickly as possible to resolve this. Adrian had canceled several appointments to stay at home, so she knew where to find him.

The carriage ride those few blocks were the longest of her life as she picked and chose which words she would use to broach the subject with her husband. After a few tries under her breath so that Fisk would not hear, she decided on an opening.

They arrived at Warfield Place and she walked into the foyer when Sherman opened the door. As Fisk took her hat and her bag to return them to her room, Miranda asked, "Sherman, is His Grace still at home?"

The butler's glance toward the study gave away the answer. She started for the door, but he reached it first. "May I announce you, Your Grace?"

"There is no need, Sherman."

He did not move quite as quickly as she wanted, so she stepped around him and opened the door herself. Adrian stood by the window.

"Windmere, I wish to speak to you, and it will not wait any longer," she said, striding toward him. "We need to clear the air between us and I want an explanation from you." She reached his side. "And I will not be put off again about this matter."

"Miranda," he said, obviously surprised by her appearance there and her manner. She followed his glance to the chair that faced away from the door, and realized he'd been speaking to someone.

"Your Grace," the woman said as she rose and curtsied.

"Mrs. Gresham, I did not know you were here." She nodded at the woman from the village at Windmere Park. "When did you arrive?" Adrian guided her to a seat as she tried to recover from being insufferably rude.

"Your Grace, I can wait outside if you must speak," Mrs. Gresham offered.

"No, Mrs. Gresham. It is I who will come back when you have finished your business with His Grace. I apologize for the intrusion, Windmere."

Before she could leave, Adrian shook his head. Meeting her gaze, he walked over to the other chair and sat down. "Actually, this might be for the best."

Now that the moment was at hand, she found that she was the one having difficulty breathing. Her stomach twisted and her head throbbed as she waited for him to speak the truth to her.

"Miranda, I have been seeking Mrs. Gresham's counsel and care for some months now. You know that she has been providing various preparations to help with my breathing problems and the attacks I am prone to." He paused and waited for her to give some sign of understanding.

"I know that, Windmere. Since that terrible attack you suffered at your club——"

"No, Miranda. I consulted with her at Windmere Park back in the spring."

Back in the spring? All paths led back to that time in the spring. She nodded, but said nothing, waiting for more information.

"I went there, to Windmere Park, after meeting with the physicians whom I have been seeing here in the city. Drs. Wilkins, Penworthy and Lloyd are among the best for various respiratory ailments, and I have been seeing one or all of them for some time—years, actually."

She clenched her hands together, struggling against the urge to scream out any number of questions and hurry him along in his explanation. He must have seen it, for he leaned forward, took her hands in his and entwined their fingers. Though such open affection in front of a visitor was unheard of, he knelt down in front of her and looked at her directly. The bile rose in her stomach. This was not good news. This felt very, very terrible.

"Miranda, the doctors agreed on one thing—my condition has worsened so much that they expect I will not live another year."

The words crashed around her and she fought against their force and power. It could not be true. He was young. He was healthy. He could not die.

"This is not possible, Adrian. I cannot believe it."

"I did not wish to, either, but as my symptoms worsened, I could not ignore the truth any longer."

She looked at their entwined hands and shook her head. "There must be a mistake. Many people suffer with the same condition you have and they do not die from it." Miranda looked at the older woman, who had such healing abilities. "Mrs. Gresham, please tell His Grace that he is mistaken about this."

Part of her knew it was futile. But another part wanted to deny that this could happen. Memories of the last several months flashed through Miranda's mind, scenes of Adrian and his illness. The medication cabinet in his room. The teas and tonics and concoctions that he drank several times each day. The small closet that had been converted for his use when inhaling the fumes of various types of burning leaves. The echoing sounds of his coughing—in the night, in the day.

"What can I tell you, ma'am? I think you know it is true. Asthma worsens with age, but the damage caused by attacks speeds up the condition, as well."

"Adrian…"

Miranda could feel the tears in her eyes and in her throat, and she blinked against them. She had plenty of time to cry. Right now they need to come up with a way to fight this. She would not lose him now that they had found so much together.

Now that she loved him.

She took in a breath and blew it out, trying not to shake with the upset. Clearing her thoughts, she looked at him and saw his concern for her in his gaze. All this time, he'd been facing death alone.

"I will not let you die, Adrian. Not now." She hesitated to admit to loving him. With all of this facing him, he did not need that additional burden.

"Miranda, I do not think we have much of a choice over the matter."

"The Almighty cannot be planning to take you from me so soon. I cannot believe He would be so small-minded as to do such a thing." Adrian laughed at that comment, but she meant it seriously. "Mrs. Gresham, there must be something we can do to improve his condition and lessen the chances of him... dying. We will do whatever is necessary, will we not, Adrian?"

"Parker said you could be my biggest help in this and I did not listen." He kissed her hands and then her mouth.

"Lord Parker knows?" It explained much now.

"He has been the best friend, Miranda. Please do not be angry with him over this."

Adrian needed as much support as possible as they searched for ways to thwart this disease, so she certainly did not begrudge him a friend in his time of need.

"I am glad he has been there for you, Adrian." She realized that they were not alone and that she'd been calling him by his Christian name. "Forgive me, Windmere."

"I am certain that you have much to discuss, so I will take my leave of you," Mrs. Gresham said. "Your Grace, I will be in the kitchen. If you can send your man to me there, I will show him these new medicaments."

"Very good, Mrs. Gresham. I thank you again for traveling so far at my request," Adrian replied.

Mrs. Gresham left, and once they were alone, Adrian pulled Miranda into his arms and kissed her. He was still before her, kneeling, when he turned them and she ended up sitting across his lap on the floor. She did not want to let go of him yet, so she wrapped her arms around him and laid her head on his chest.

"We have much to talk about, but I would rather not do it here," he murmured.

"The servants will be discreet, Adrian. Do you not trust them?"

"I would keep this among as few people as possible. The servants are well aware of my illness, but I do not wish them to know the rest. Word of the duke's impending death would have many consequences, and I would rather control it as long as I am able."

Consequences she had not even considered yet, the news being so fresh that it did not seem real to her. So many questions formed in her mind and she wanted answers to all of them.

"Where should we go then?" she asked. Shifting on his lap, she tried to regain her feet, without success. He held her waist and lifted her until she could stand.

"A walk in the park would be just the thing."

Adrian rang for Sherman who called for their carriage. As they drove through the paths around the Serpentine Pool in Hyde Park, he explained the intricacies of his affliction and the treatments he'd endured to lessen the symptoms and to stave off the apparently in-evitable outcome. It was a long time before her tears calmed and Miranda found herself grateful for Adrian's attempt to spare her from the embarrassment of being witnessed in this highly emotional state.

Chapter Seventeen

The next month reminded Miranda of a sketch she'd seen once of the famous Seven Hills of Rome. It was a small drawing, with the hills out of proper perspective so they appeared much closer together than they should have. Being in a coach, going at a full gallop up and down those hills, would describe her life once Adrian had delivered the news to her.

So many things became clear to her as she considered the information. He admitted to being influenced by the doctors' prognosis into adjusting his life, and part of that had been seeing her in a different light. He was candid about his desire for an heir, one that he might not ever know, but who could continue his work. He confessed that his impending death was the catalyst that had changed their relationship.

He would not discuss many of the issues regarding the ducal estates, but she gathered he had a number of reasons for not wanting his distant cousin to inherit. Uncomfortable with such details, he assured her that, in the event of his death without an heir, all was in order.

The subject of an heir was not openly discussed after that, but now she understood the facts that compelled him to seek medical advice about her delay in conceiving. And though she knew that most all of his reasons for wanting a child centered on the needs of his family and his titles, hers was now based on a simple one—she wanted something of him in the event, the very small chance, that the physicians were correct about his condition.

A son with his smile. And with his eyes, the color of which changed with his mood or the weather, sometimes appearing a pale brown with hints of green, at other times a striking gold with flashes of brown. She decided she would like to have a son who looked back at her with those eyes.

Even though the attacks of coughing came more often and sometimes were terrifying, Miranda and Adrian loved. Well, she whispered words of love to him in her mind as he made her scream with pleasure, but she did not say them aloud. Adrian was attentive and supportive of her when desperation overcame her and she could not hold it in. Some nights they simply held each other and talked until morning. Other nights, and sometimes even in the light of day, he was relentless in his attentions to her.

After the initial shock, and although she was tempted to withdraw to the house and keep to themselves, they tried to put up a normal facade of appearances and attendances. Miranda continued to act as chaperon for Miss Stevenson, and the dowager's goddaughter even accompanied them on a short trip to Bath so that Adrian could take the waters there. And although Sophie asked searching questions and constantly looked at her with a worried expression, Miranda honored Adrian's request not to share the dreadfulness of the situation.

Juliet's Romeo followed not long after their departure from London, and the foursome actually enjoyed the sights and pleasures that the city of Bath had to offer. It being the low season, there were no crowds to fight to enjoy tea in the Pump Room or a picnic luncheon on the park in front of the Royal Crescent.

When Adrian's breathing became markedly improved during a foray to Bristol, Miranda agreed that the seashore would be ideal for an extended visit. They returned to London to make arrangements for finishing the summer in Brighton. Although she dreaded facing the influx of the ton there due to the Regent's frequent presence, Miranda would do anything if it meant a chance for Adrian's improvement.

Their weeks in Brighton, filled with bathing in the ocean and walking on the promenade and on the beach, came to an end too soon for her tastes. She knew that Adrian had many responsibilities as the Duke of Windmere, but she dreaded returning to the city. Finally, when July turned into August and the end of the Season was in sight, they were back in residence.

Knowing that the autumn would be upon them soon and that the doctors' prognosis was vague, she felt tension growing within her. Her sleep was troubled by nightmares, her appetite was off and she seemed less and less able to keep her emotions at bay. After weeks of being strong for him, Miranda could feel her control over her feelings slipping away. But if she seemed a bit sensitive or different, she told herself, the nervous tension of her life was certainly the reason.

"Your behavior is becoming obvious, Windmere." Parker took a drink of port and sat down next to him.

Adrian and Miranda had been back in town for two weeks and he had lost no time in attempting to find her next husband. After discussing some issues of a personal nature with Mrs. Gresham outside his wife's presence or knowledge, he'd changed his course of therapy, medications and tonics. Although the new regimen might prove to have other benefits, it was not as effective in preventing the attacks as the previous one. Time was running out for him, for them, and he took the risks he needed to succeed.

"Whatever do you mean, Parker? Are they discussing the changes in my health?"

"No, damn you. They are asking if you are offering places in your wife's bed as well as at her table and in her theater box."

"Give me the names of those who have uttered such insults!"

"And what will you do? Have a morning appointment with each of them? To what avail?"

"Why are you so angry over this?"

"Because it is the wrong thing to do. I understand the need to see to things like the house and the income, but finding her a husband? Adrian, this will bring her reputation into question and may undermine everything you are trying to do."

He thought on Will's words. For months now, he'd felt much as a fox in a hunt did. He could hear the approaching hounds barking, even feel their bite as they nipped at his ankles, while he tried to make preparations for what would come. After years of gathering the power of his position and titles into his hands, this had happened and sent him spinning. Here he had no control, no power, and nothing—not his wealth or his estates or his businesses—could provide him a way to buy out of it.

"Perhaps I have gone a bit far," he admitted softly. "I worry so about the duchess's life after this."

"Adrian, you have friends. The duchess has friends. They will not abandon her, especially not after…well, you know."

"I would hope not," he replied.

"Besides, who knows what fate has in store for you? I am still planning to have you stand for me at my wedding."

"From your mouth to the Almighty's ears. May he listen to you, since he is not busy listening to me."

Adrian's chest tightened and a few coughs bubbled up. The club's drawing room grew silent, with many of the occupants watching him out of the corner of their eye. When the spell passed and he breathed again, everyone turned back to their own concerns.

"The coughing seems on the increase again. Are Mrs. Gresham's tonics no longer effective?"

"We are trying something different."

"And have you seen the doctors again? Have they any suggestions?"

"I have not seen them in months. Mrs. Gresham's advice has been more sound."

"Until now," Parker added.

"Until now," he confirmed. Of course, he knew it was not the woman's fault. Most likely the changes he had dictated to her recommendations were the reason for his recent decline, and they were his choice for the time being.

"I must meet my father at Tatt's in a bit," Parker said, finishing his port. "Are you going to give up on this foolhardy venture?"

Adrian nodded. "I think so. You make much sense with your words."

He had not thought about the possible ramifications to Miranda's reputation if this was seen as something dishonorable. He had planned to be discreet, both in searching for possible candidates and in making an offer, but the pressure on him had forced his hand somewhat in the timing of it.

"The house is done?"

"Nearly," he replied.

After much searching, Adrian had located a newer neighborhood on the outskirts of London that was drawing the type of people whom Miranda might be comfortable living around. It was far enough from the frenzy and close enough to the countryside she seemed to favor.

"A few more weeks and it will be ready. Then, at least, she will have a choice when the matter comes to a conclusion."

"Then will you sit back and enjoy the time you have?" Parker stood and shook his hand. "I still believe it is not over yet."

Adrian watched his friend walk away, then turn back.

"I almost forgot to tell you. Caro is home from her trip abroad and wants a few minutes of your time. Some news to share, she said."

"Caro? I have not spoken to her since…"

"Right. She said to tell you she'll be at the fireworks at Vauxhall tomorrow evening, if it is convenient."

They had not spoken since he'd broken off with her the night after he'd found out the news about his health. He'd heard she'd left on an extended trip, probably using the money he'd given her as a parting gift. What ever could she want to speak to him about?

Parker went off and Adrian sat for a while considering all the reasons that his former mistress could want to see him. Did she seek to return to his protection? What news could she bear him?

Well, tomorrow was not so far away, and he had no

plans, since Miranda was scheduled to spend the evening at Lady Allendale's, with Miss Stevenson in tow. He'd not asked, but he knew the time and place to meet Caro. Their usual arrangements—ten in the evening, next to the statue of Aphrodite.

"I cannot believe I let you convince me to do this!" Miranda said, laughing at Sophie as they walked along a path at Vauxhall Gardens. Thirsty after laughing and applauding the last fireworks show planned for the Season, they were on their way now to enjoy some ices at one of the pavilions.

"Sometimes, things done on the fly can be the most fun," Sophie replied. "Besides, with my husband here, we are more than adequately chaperoned for the protection of Miss Stevenson's reputation."

Juliet's bright eyes and smile told of her excitement at being included in such plans. The young woman, whose appearance and mannerisms were flawlessly polite, turned her head this way and that taking in all the sights. The perfect English beauty, with her ice blue eyes and pale blond hair, never made any misstep as Miranda had in those first days and weeks in society. Even now, Miranda could hear the rebuke that the dowager would offer for such behavior.

The dowager made her disapproval of such a place quite clear, and so Miss Stevenson's mother never dared let the girl go. Miranda had attended once or twice with Adrian and saw nothing harmful, if one stayed in the public areas and did not pursue the darkened corners and alcoves scattered along the paths.

When Sophie suggested it, Miranda could see that the young woman simply wanted a chance to find what drew so much attention from the ton. They all agreed that the presence and escort of Lord and Lady Allendale, as well as the Duchess of Windmere, would squelch any gossip.

The night was pleasantly cool, and they walked along, enjoying the sights and the music. Lord Allendale escorted them to a table and ordered refreshments.

Miranda was just settling in her seat when she glanced up and saw a familiar figure. Adrian was here! She would have missed him if she'd turned a moment later.

She watched as he walked around the pavilion where they were seated and headed off. He must have called for her at the Allendales' and been told they were here. Miranda stood and excused herself to gain his attention.

He was faster than her, and then she saw him step off the path near one of the larger statues of the various Greek gods and goddesses. She'd almost reached the same clearing when his voice rang out.

"Caro!"

Her husband's former mistress smiled and walked up to him. He opened his arms and took her into his embrace. They looked at each other and then he kissed her. On the mouth.

"Come, let's walk somewhere more private."

With that, she watched in horrified silence as Adrian

walked off with that woman. Judging from the warm welcome and the kiss and embrace, they were still on good terms.

Very good terms.

Miranda stood alone, staring off along the darkened path where they had gone, unable to think about the scene she had witnessed. A sound behind her alerted her to someone else's presence. She turned and found Lord Allendale there. From the expression on his face, he, too, had seen the tête-à-tête.

"Sophie was worried that you were going alone. She asked me to follow you, to escort you."

All Miranda could do was nod and accept his arm. Stunned, she walked at his side until they reached Sophie and Miss Stevenson. It took her friend less than a minute to realize something was wrong. When pressed, Miranda could think of nothing to say.

"I fear that Her Grace stumbled on the path and may have twisted her ankle," Lord Allendale announced to his wife. "I suggest that we make our way back to the carriage and take her home."

Sophie murmured all the correct phrases, but did not believe a word of her husband's explanation, Miranda knew. She allowed it to continue because there was no choice. Meanwhile Miranda clung to Lord Allendale's arm for support, not having to pretend, for now that the shock had hit her, she discovered her legs were not holding her up well enough on their own.

Her husband was meeting with his former mistress.

What reason could there be for it, save one? Were they rekindling their involvement? Why now? The thoughts churned in her mind, and each time, all she could see was that kiss and that embrace.

The Allendale coach rolled across the Thames into Mayfair, taking her back to her house.

Her husband, she knew, would not be waiting up for her.

"Caro!" he said, as she approached. He felt genuine affection when he saw her, for they had been both good friends and lovers. Opening his arms, he embraced her and kissed her in welcome. "Come, let's walk somewhere more private than here."

He took her by the hand and led her down the path to a secluded bench. Once they were seated, she leaned over and kissed him again. He accepted it, but whatever passion had been between them was gone now. Loving Miranda as he did made it impossible to feel the same toward another woman, especially one in his past.

"So, it is true, then?" she said, squinting at him as she watched him.

"What is true?"

"I heard two rumors on my return to London this week, and both involved you. I thought it best to find out the truth from the source. Especially considering our past."

"And the rumors?" he asked. He thought she may have heard about his worsening health, but could not think of what the other one might be.

She released his hand and looked into his eyes. She was a stunning beauty, with emerald-green eyes and porcelain skin. Her long blond hair was arranged in some new style, but the length of it hung down over her shoulder and rested on her bosom. Her not inconsiderable bosom.

But she was not Miranda.

"That you are in love with your wife," she said, smiling. "No need to answer, for I could tell the moment you kissed me that it was true."

"You could?"

"It was a polite kiss, Adrian. Warm even, but not passionate, as the ones we used to share. It is your wife, is it not?"

"Yes. Things have changed between the duchess and me," he admitted. "But that was not until after you and I had parted ways." He laughed then, feeling very strange at the thought of being unfaithful to his mistress.

"Strange, eh? Did the duchess know about us?"

"Yes, it turns out that she did. Much more than I ever realized." He thought back to the things Miranda had told him that day at Windmere Park. He glanced back at Caro. "And the other rumor?"

A frown marred her brow and she took his hand again. "I have heard that your health has worsened. Is it true?"

"It is, Caro. But I am under treatment and expect things will work out." He smiled at her and she searched his face.

"You always promised that you would not lie to me, and I appreciated that far more than you will even know, Adrian. Why are you lying now?"

She had always had the ability to read him—his moods, his desires, his needs. He should have known better than to try to fool her. He met her gaze and then looked away.

"It is bad. Not much more to say than that."

Her eyes filled with tears, and Adrian found that more difficult to face than many other situations he'd experienced. She leaned against his arm, wrapping hers around him and putting her head on his shoulder.

"And the duchess knows?" she asked a few minutes later.

"Yes, she knows," he said, now feeling guilty over the delay in telling Miranda. "And she has been a wonderful help to me. Caro, I have the best physicians treating me."

"Good. I am glad things have worked out between you. She was always polite to me."

"To you? When did you meet her?" He was not aware that the two women had ever met.

"We have seen each other a few times at places in town. Once at Clark & Debenham's shop. Another time at the subscription library on New Bond Street. Only in passing, of course, but she never cut me as her friends do."

Miranda would never cease to offer him surprises. Her behavior, her personality—everything about her amazed him.

Caro sat up and smoothed her gown. "I am glad she is at your side through whatever you are facing." His ex-mistress stood and he did as well.

"Parker said you had some news to share with me?"

"Yes, and then I must leave. Actually, could you walk me to my carriage?"

He held out his arm and they walked toward a different entrance to the Gardens, one frequently used by those not wishing to be witnessed.

"I wanted to tell you personally that I am to be married soon."

He stopped and looked at her in surprise. "Married? I thought you swore off that state with the death of Mr. Robinson?"

"I did. At least I swore I would not marry someone I did not love."

"So, this means you are in love? Who is the man?" He stopped and looked at her in surprise. The always pragmatic Mrs. Robinson in love?

"An American, if you can believe it! We met in Brussels and things have progressed between us. His offer of marriage came only this week."

"And is he honorable? Where will you live?" Adrian felt more like an older brother concerned over a sister's interests. Strange, that, for their affair had been quite passionate.

"He has a business in Pennsylvania, in Philadelphia, and we will live there. I just wanted to be certain that I could offer him my heart." They walked on, nearing the line of carriages. She indicated hers and he escorted her to it.

"This was a test, then?"

"I fear so."

"And did we pass or fail?" He knew the state of his own heart and in whose possession it lay.

"I think we passed, for it seems we have both discovered love."

"Just so." He nodded in agreement. "You know that you can call on me if there is need."

They reached her carriage and the groom opened the door. Adrian took her hand and kissed it. "You have my best wishes, Mrs. Robinson."

He handed her up, and once she was settled, she turned back to him. "And I am always your servant, Your Grace."

The groom closed the door and climbed up behind to his place. The driver shook the reins and the carriage rolled on. Adrian's own gig was nearby and the drive home uneventful. He was met at the door with the news that the duchess was indisposed, so after checking in on her, he drank the various required concoctions and sought sleep in his own bed.

Chapter Eighteen

After four days of not feeling well, Miranda decided that redecorating would lift her spirits. Adrian had not mentioned that evening to her, and she was waiting for him to do so.

Although Sophie had come up with all sorts of possible explanations for what she had seen at Vauxhall, all Miranda had to do was ask her friend her husband's opinion and Sophie became quiet. Lord Allendale never spoke of the incident to Miranda, but his expression that night had told her exactly what she feared the most.

She was not certain when Adrian would return to her bed, but so far he had accepted her excuse of being indisposed. She heard him open her door each night and then proceed on to his own. Before, when she did not love him, she'd been resigned to sharing his attentions with another woman. It was, as so many had explained to her, the way it was done. Now, after gaining his attentions and, she'd thought, his love, she would find it impossible to go back to living like that.

Looking for a distraction from her uncertainty, Miranda opened the storage closet and searched through the watercolors stored there. She was looking for a particular painting, one she'd done for him after their trip to Brighton. He'd laughed when she chose to paint a picture of the large yellow flowers that grew near the house they'd rented. If he could not smell them, at least he could be around them, she'd explained at the time. Now, with her spirits crumbling, she hoped it would cheer up the drawing room and her.

"Mrs. Manning, I do not see the painting I'm looking for in here. Where else do you have them stored?" The housekeeper was following her from closet to closet as she searched.

"This is the only place, ma'am. The other closet is not dry enough to trust them."

"That is very strange. It is one of my newest paintings."

"Your Grace, Meg said that His Grace has it."

"The duke? Is it in his chambers? Or in his study?" Miranda dusted off her dress, closed the door and waited for an answer from the chambermaid.

"It is not in his room, Your Grace. I just cleaned there and there's no painting of yellow flowers there," the girl said.

Miranda waved them off and walked downstairs to Adrian's study. She'd been in here a few days ago and had not seen it. Sherman opened the door for her and she dismissed him to other duties.

As she'd thought, no new watercolors were hanging here. Walking around the desk, she looked to see if it was anywhere else in the room. That was when she saw the papers on the desktop, spilling from a leather portfolio. She only recognized them because of the names; it was the list of possible suitors for Miss Stevenson that she and Adrian had reviewed. The same men with whom she'd found herself dancing and eating and watching a play and walking and…

Curious, she pulled out the sheets of paper and looked more carefully at them. The list, with only Lord Parker's name crossed out, included not only their names and her general comments, but more notes scratched around the margins and facts underlined in her husband's own hand. Financial information, their worth, their yearly incomes, and another figure that she thought might be their indebtedness. Family connections and names of their friends and business associates were scribbled as well.

Miranda sat down and read the information several times. This did not make sense. Then she noticed the comments on the second sheet. Next to each man's name was a list of her own social engagements and which of the men she'd met or spoken to or shared a meal or other situation with. If she had been given only this information, it could have been damning to her reputation, but she knew that her husband had been present at each one. Indeed, he had brought about the introductions and released her into the company of these men each time.

Her stomach churned as she tried to figure out the reasons for this bizarre list. Why would he keep track of such things? Even more, why would he seemingly plan such interactions between his wife and these men?

Miranda opened the portfolio to see if there was something that could help her understand his notes. A letter from Dr. Blake was there. The message was short and to the point—"for your use"—and his signature. The other document was longer, filled with medical terms and details of his visit and his consultation about her lack of fertility. She gasped when she read his declaration that, in his professional opinion, she was unable to have children and would be unable to do so.

Adrian had alluded to it, but had never said how negative Dr. Blake's opinion had been. And this document, a report for the duke's use, stated it in no uncertain terms—she was barren.

The tears fell before she even knew she was crying, and she leaned back so that they did not fall on his papers. There was no hope of a child, according to the doctor's words. *Any efforts to beget an heir will be met with failure due to the duchess's infertile womb.*

Waves of nausea passed over her as she sat there thinking about and crying over what she'd read. And when she remembered the sight of Adrian and his mistress meeting, it was all she could take. She barely made it to the downstairs water closet before her stomach rebelled completely.

With her head pounding and her stomach still unsettled, she knew she must confront Adrian about these strange occurrences. He would explain it and all would be well. She sought the comfort of her bed for a short rest and was almost there when Sherman approached her with a note.

Almost afraid to read the words, she allowed Fisk to help her undress and put on a robe before opening it. Sitting on the edge of her bed, she read it.

Madam—
I hope you are well.
Business calls me away for at most two days.
Contact me through Webb if you need anything.
Yours—W

It was just as well that he did not come home. It would take a day or so for her to regain her calm and face her husband with all the questions racing through her mind. She fell into a light sleep, but woke a few hours later feeling worse. After a simple meal, she retired to her room and read for the rest of the evening.

She begged off from an afternoon engagement she'd planned with Sophie, and found herself wandering through the house and gardens, then back to Adrian's study. The papers made little more sense to her now than they had the first ten times she'd read them. Tempted to show them to Sophie, she decided against it. She would give Adrian a chance to explain them first.

Just before dinner, she received a note from Lady Allendale. The urgency in the words forced her to answer her friend's summons. Dreading whatever Sophie had discovered with her formidable network of gossip and news, she dressed and went to call on her. Not sure that she was ready to hear the truth, but unwilling to live a lie, she waited for the information that she feared would end the loving marriage she'd sought for so long with her husband.

Their talk went on and Sophie had learned much about Adrian's actions of the last several days and weeks, and each fact cut Miranda's heart into pieces.

Mrs. Caro Robinson was back in London and had been seen by many in the duke's company at Vauxhall that night. A rather costly gift of crystal had been sent to the hotel where she was staying, with a card written by the duke himself.

A Mr. Adrian Warfield had opened several accounts with various shops that were providing furniture, linens and other supplies necessary to stocking and decorating a house.

The same Mr. Adrian Warfield had purchased a house in a new section of a London suburb.

Miranda refused to believe it. Her heart simply would not accept that he was seeing his mistress again, but the proof was there in front of her when she made Sophie drive with her to the address given as the new house. In a carriage that could not be identified as the viscountess's, they drove past Number 60 on the fashionable new street.

The house was not complete yet, but it had occupants whom she could see through an undraped window in the front. As their carriage moved down the street, Miranda leaned closer and peered into the house.

Adrian stood in the center of the room, pointing at various objects and speaking to someone she could not see immediately. Then he moved out of her view and she glimpsed Lord Parker. Although the house itself was enough to make her husband's intentions clear, and his presence here another insult to her, at least there was no woman with him.

Shaking her head at Sophie's offer to stop and accompany her to speak to her husband, Miranda discovered that she did not have the courage to do so at that moment. She racked her brain for reasons for Adrian buying a house that did not involve some discreet liaison of a personal nature, but she could not come up with one. Even while acting as devil's advocate for a moment, Sophie was stymied by the question.

Deciding to pursue this when he returned home, Miranda rapped on the roof to tell the driver to move on, just as a coach approached from the other direction. Leaning back so that they could not be seen, Miranda nevertheless was able to view the occupant in the other vehicle.

Mrs. Caro Robinson.

Wordlessly, both she and Sophie turned and watched the carriage stop at the house they had just passed. With help from the groom, the woman climbed out and was greeted by Adrian.

Together, they walked into Number 60 Charleston Street.

Sophie wrapped her arm around Miranda and held her as they drove back to the Allendale house. Unable to believe what they'd seen, and knowing that Adrian would not be home, Miranda allowed Sophie to send word to Warfield Place that she would be staying the night with the viscountess. After a glass of very good brandy, Miranda found herself bundled off to bed. Still awake at dawn, she contemplated what the rest of her life would be like, first facing his infidelity and then his death.

Adrian returned to Warfield Place and was surprised to find that Miranda was gone. Sherman informed him that the duchess had sent word from Lady Allendale's that she was spending the night there. When he checked her appointment and invitation book, he found there was nothing scheduled for the next several days.

Once the decorators finished the house, he wanted to take her there and show it to her. He and Parker had argued over that, too, but Caro had settled the question. He'd asked her there for a woman's opinion of the location and the house itself, and she'd sided with him about when to tell the duchess.

Going to his study, he found the portfolio of papers

on his desk and thought about his plan to find a husband for her. He had not remembered leaving them out so plainly on his desk. Looking over his notes, he smiled at what her reaction might be to such a scheme. Part of him was curious about which man she would have chosen. Then he realized that, after his death, at least she would know these men if one or more did indeed become suitors for her.

After destroying the papers and the odious and doubtful report from Dr. Blake, Adrian decided to turn in early. By habit, his feet stopped at her door, even though he knew she was not at home. Opening it, he breathed in the scent of her from the room.

Footsteps in the hallway stopped behind him.

"Your Grace," a woman said.

"Good evening, Fisk."

"I wondered if the duchess is well?"

Adrian faced his wife's maid. "Why would you think otherwise?"

He knew she had been ill for a few days, and related that to her monthly. With all their efforts on producing an heir, Miranda tended to be rather glum when it came and revealed that they had not been successful.

"The duchess had a rather restless night, sir. And she did not look well when she went to Lady Allendale's."

"Her message said nothing of being ill, did it?"

"No, sir."

"Then I am certain she will return in the morning as

fit as always." He closed the bedroom door. "Good night, Fisk."

"Good night, Your Grace."

The encounter disturbed him. Miranda had been the strong one in these last few months. If nervous tension could worsen his own condition, he had no doubt that it could affect other illnesses.

But once they retired to Windmere Park, things would calm for both of them. As he'd promised Parker, after all the arrangements were finalized, he would step back and simply live the rest of his life with his wife, however long that was.

The morning came abruptly when he was awakened with word of serious problems at Windmere Park. A fire, the message said, had destroyed several buildings, and he was needed at once. As Thompson packed his things, Adrian sent word with a footman to Miranda.

Unfortunately, the footman chosen to deliver the message took it instead to the other Duchess of Windmere. The dowager managed to keep several Warfield Place servants on her payroll so that she was kept apprised of activities in the household. The note was altered at the dowager's order and then delivered to the Allendales' guest.

Having sent the original note to her son, she knew her path was clear to handle the family's biggest problem without interference. Cordelia sat back and waited for the duchess to arrive back home and receive her call. She had waited long enough to dispose of this unacceptable wife.

By the time her son traveled north to Windmere Park, ascertained that there was no emergency, and returned to London, Miranda would be gone and Windmere would be free to seek another wife. A young and fertile one, a woman who would listen to the guidance of her betters and her elders, a woman who would be grateful to Cordelia for all she received.

A woman like Juliet.

Chapter Nineteen

Sherman announced the dowager's arrival at exactly two o'clock, the time she'd specified in her note the day before. Still surprised by Adrian's request that she meet with the dowager, Miranda was waiting in the drawing room. Cordelia entered the room as she always did, head held high and looking down her nose. Although tempted to remain seated, Miranda stood and offered a welcome to Adrian's mother.

"Your Grace," she said, then she sat down and waved the butler over to serve tea and cakes.

"Miranda," the dowager replied. "As I mentioned in my note to you, this is not a social call. Take the refreshments away, Sherman."

The butler looked to Miranda before obeying the blatant and inappropriate order.

"I would like some tea, Sherman. Then you may take the rest away." She felt a petty satisfaction from countermanding the dowager, but this was her home and it was her place to order the servants about if need be.

He poured the tea, added the amount of sugar she preferred and then handed it to her. "Will there be anything else, ma'am?" he asked.

"Leave us!" Cordelia ordered.

Surprised at her blatant rudeness, Miranda shook her head. "No, thank you, Sherman. You may all go." He and the under butler and Fisk left the room, and Sherman closed the door behind them. She turned to face the older woman.

"You seem to be very agitated, Your Grace. Is there some problem?"

"The matter we have to discuss is of the utmost importance to the Windmere name, and I do not want to dawdle over drinking tea or coddling the servants. My son…"

"I did not know you were on speaking terms with your son. His last orders to me were that I should not meet with you without him present." Trying to stay in control, she sipped her tea. "Until his note, of course, and yours."

"Windmere trusts my discretion, and what we must discuss is extremely personal in nature. As his note indicated, he asked me to speak to you in this delicate matter. And he had given me permission, power even, to make certain arrangements on his behalf."

Icy fingers ran up and down Miranda's spine as the dowager spoke. Adrian allowing his mother to represent him? This did not sound right to her, but she waited to discover the real reason for this visit.

"I am his wife and the Duchess of Windmere, madam. What kind of arrangements can he want *you* to make?"

"You are not a stupid woman, Miranda, although certain of your actions have been questionable in the last few months. I am sure you know what I need to speak to you about."

Miranda had not noticed the package the dowager had carried in with her until now. Opening it, Cordelia pulled out a familiar looking piece of paper and handed it to her. Dr. Blake's report, although this one looked slightly different than the one she'd seen on Adrian's desk.

"Have you seen this?" she asked.

"I have."

"Then you know the eminent doctor's findings. You will never bear a child and cannot fulfill your duties as Duchess of Windmere."

"Physicians can be wrong, Your Grace. As yours was about Adrian's treatment that night."

"But the proof is here for all to see, Miranda. Seven years of marriage and not any results. I know the duke has been favoring you with much more attention these last few months, to no avail. Even sharing his bed has not helped."

Miranda gasped. How could she know these things?

"He decided a few months ago to let his mistress go and concentrate on gaining a son. In spite of it, you have not conceived. Indeed, as the doctor concludes, your womb will never give him an heir."

She was mixing different situations and making

it sound terrible. "That is not why he quit seeing her. He—"

Miranda stopped herself before the words spilled out. Adrian specifically did not want his mother to know of his health situation.

"Ah, yes, he did not stop seeing her completely. As a matter of fact, he called her back just a few weeks ago. He is tired of the farce he tried to maintain with you."

"Farce? What farce?"

Cordelia's face softened and she offered Miranda a look of sympathy. "As I tried to make you understand, men of his position and power need the diversion of other women to satisfy those more exotic desires they have. He was contented to spend himself on you while he thought you would produce a son, but your appeal has lessened with each passing month. Mrs. Robinson offers those diversions to him. Now that he has bought that house for her, there will be no need for him to frequent your fruitless bed."

Miranda could not believe any of this. Yes, Adrian had bought the house for that woman, but it still did not make sense. His mother was twisting the facts for her own reasons. Miranda could not think that all of these months he had been dishonest. She clasped her hands together to keep them from shaking. This did not make sense!

"Adrian loves me and I love him. You are lying…."

Cordelia leaned back and laughed at her words. Miranda could not ever remember the dowager doing such a thing.

"My dear, for five years I tried to counsel you about the role into which you married. Love has nothing to do with this union. Certainly, it is difficult to have such a vigorous physical relationship with someone without some tender feelings, but men of Windmere's class do not love their wives."

Cordelia stood and walked over to her. "Men such as Windmere marry for money and power and titles and sons. And that is the crux of this problem. *Your* problem. If you cannot give him a son, you are not needed. He stood courageously by you for some seven years without blaming you." The dowager placed her hand on Miranda's shoulder and patted it.

This was almost too easy, she thought. The girl was crumbling before her eyes and she'd seen only the first of many papers prepared for this. It was another reason the marriage must end, another sign of the gel's unworthiness to continue to carry the Windmere name.

"There are two ways that we can escape this travesty, and Windmere has authorized me to offer you both. Because of your physical condition, our solicitor has suggested the best way is to seek an annulment of the marriage."

The girl blinked and gasped. "An annulment? But we have been married for seven years, and certainly it has been consummated. There would be no grounds for an annulment."

Cordelia sat again and nodded. "Generally, that might be correct. But the solicitor informed us that there is a section of ecclesiastical law which equates sterility with impotence, and so both are grounds for an annulment. With the medical opinion of such a eminent physician stating so, and your cooperation, of course, this would be the quietest way to accomplish an end to the marriage and allow each of you to remarry. If you choose to, that is."

"This is wrong. You are wrong. I cannot believe that Adrian would want me to do something like this."

She could see the girl's control slipping, and the doubts she was feeding her were working their way into her thoughts. "It is a difficult thing to do, Miranda, but much easier for all concerned than our other option. With an annulment, you would simply have to sign some papers and possibly submit to another examination. Privately, of course." She paused until she had Miranda's complete attention. "There is so much more involved in petitioning for a divorce."

"Divorce," she cried out. Then, lowering her voice, she stated, "There are no grounds for divorce."

"Generally, the grounds are adultery and they are granted with certain proof being provided." Cordelia reached into the portfolio of papers and drew out reports from the investigators she'd hired. "Now, I cannot believe that you have been involved in debauchery and lascivious behavior with all of these men, but the reports seem to indicate that you have."

Shaking her head in denial, Miranda reached out and took the pile of reports. She did not need to know that her investigators could rival the greatest writers of fiction in the last century, Cordelia decided. Not giving the chit time to examine them closely, she took the next step. "It does not seem fair that Windmere will not be considered responsible for his liaison with Mrs. Robinson, but in the eyes of the law and the courts, women are held to a much higher standard of acceptable behavior."

"These," shaking the papers in her hand, Miranda cried out, "are not true. Adrian was there at each of those encounters and will say so. He introduced those men to me and…" She drifted off, likely realizing that she'd damned him with her own words.

"Just so, my dear. And you will be held responsible for those *encounters* as you call them."

Right when she thought Miranda's capitulation was at hand, the girl demonstrated backbone Cordelia had not seen before.

"These are all lies. The papers, the investigators, even your suggestion that you do this at Adrian's bidding." Miranda stood and paced the room. "And how convenient for you that he is halfway to northern England and cannot be asked to corroborate your words."

"Are you saying that I am lying? Call my bluff then and see if he comes to your rescue. Or if he *conveniently* is out of town for the worst of the scandal that will be caused by your refusal to come to some agreeable arrangements. Do not force his solicitors to step in and deal with you."

"I cannot imagine why you would do something so

horrible to me, Cordelia. I have done nothing for the last eight years but provide a dowry to save your estates, marry your son and live in every way as you instructed me. What have I done to make you hate me so?" she asked, shaking her head.

The reason percolated just beneath her thoughts, but the dowager would not reveal it to this chit. "I do not hate you, my dear. In fact, I pity you for not being able to do what a true woman can do—produce a child for her husband. You will never know the joy of giving birth as I have. I pity you, Miranda. I don't hate you."

Completely inappropriately, the girl smiled at her and wiped away the tears that streamed down her cheeks. "You hate me because I have the one thing you could never claim, Cordelia. I have the love of my husband, and you cannot bear it. The old duke never loved you. He could barely tolerate you, as I understand it. And when you see what has happened between Adrian and me in spite of your efforts to the contrary, you cannot stand it. If he is involved with this, it is because of your poison. He loves me, Cordelia. Just remember that during all of your manipulations."

She sat up straighter and glared at the girl. "I did not give you permission to use my Christian name. And since you will be leaving the family soon, I do not do so now."

"There is one thing you do not know about Adrian, or you would not so foolishly have tried this."

"Now you are bluffing," she said. "My son keeps me completely informed in spite of appearances. He sent me the doctor's report after we discussed a possible divorce in his study." Keeping as close to the truth as possible in one's fabrications was pivotal, she knew.

Miranda sat down across from her and gave her a look of such pity that Cordelia almost cursed aloud. Shaking her head again, she spoke—with a confidence that made Cordelia slightly nervous.

"Although Adrian asked me not to speak of this to you, I think you should know the truth. As his mother, you should hear this from him, but your actions have given me no other choice." Miranda reached over and finished the rest of her tea. "Even if he does not love me, and even if his mistress has returned to her place in his life, the reason that Adrian will not seek a divorce or an annulment is that he cannot." She took a breath and let it out. "He does not have the time to pursue something as lengthy as those proceedings. He has, at most, only a few months to live."

Cordelia had to admit that the girl was good. Calling her bluff in this way made her feel a touch of pride and a bit disappointed that Miranda could not bear an heir for her son. She clapped her hands in appreciation of the effort, well made if misguided and wrong.

"Three of the top physicians gave him the prognosis, each one a specialist in respiratory diseases and conditions. His asthmatic condition is worsening, has worsened, to the point that they told him in the spring that he would probably not live out the year."

"Their names?" Cordelia asked, narrowing her gaze.

"Drs. Wilkins, Lloyd and Penworthy."

"You are bluffing now, for they are in my employ and would have informed me of any such dire prediction."

Miranda could see the dowager's hands trembling, and it gave her hope. And hearing that Cordelia paid these doctors, she wondered who else was being paid to provide information about their private lives. How else could Adrian's mother know so many details?

Miranda walked to the door and opened it, calling out to Sherman. "Is Mr. Webb available or has he accompanied the duke to Windmere Park?"

"He left with His Grace. His assistant, Mr. Taylor, is in his office, ma'am," the butler said.

"Call him here, if you please, Sherman. Immediately."

Within the few minutes it took her to write the doctors' names and directions down, the tall, young man reported to her. He stepped into the room and bowed. "Your Grace? How can I be of service?"

"Take the dowager's coach and bring these men back here immediately. Tell them that it is a matter of the utmost importance and urgency. Do not let them refuse, Mr. Taylor. Do you understand?"

"Yes, Your Grace," he replied, taking the note from her. "Immediately."

He left, and Miranda knew the only thing that she could do was wait. She took the package of papers now and sat as far from the dowager as she could get before beginning to read them. She was so upset by the information included in them that she had to stop several times. The dowager had done her work well, and to someone not familiar with her or Adrian, every lie she told would seem true.

The commotion in the hallway outside the room told her that the doctors had arrived, and it was finally time to put the dowager in her place. Miranda stood to greet them. As Sherman announced them, they removed their hats and bowed to her and Adrian's mother. Then they greeted the dowager personally, and it did appear as though they knew her.

"Doctors, please forgive me for interrupting your schedules with this unusual request."

"Command was more like it! Your man gave us no choice but to come," the one with the bushy eyebrows, Penworthy, said.

"How can we be of service to you, Your Grace? Ma'am?" the older one asked, looking at each of them.

"His Grace, the Duke of Windmere, was called away on an emergency, before he could explain the details of his illness to Her Grace. Would you be so kind as to tell her your prognosis?"

Miranda had never spoken to the doctors directly, so she wanted to hear this, as well. Adrian did not always have confidence in them, so another explanation might reveal something to her that could help his condition.

"Our prognosis? His Grace suffers from an asthmatic condition of the lungs, ma'am. When we last examined him, that was..." Dr. Lloyd paused.

"It has been a number of months since we saw him," Penworthy continued.

"We saw him back in April. Came here to his home and consulted with him about the coughing and the spasms of the chest," Wilkins finished.

"Had his condition worsened at that time?" Miranda asked.

"He reported an increase in symptoms, but we could find no changes in his lungs."

"No changes?" she asked. "And the advice you gave him?"

"We suggested some alterations to the medications he took, and that he should take the waters to ease the tightness in his chest."

This did not sound serious at all. Adrian had told her that they'd predicted his death. Before she could ask, Cordelia did.

"Did you inform my son that his illness had worsened to the point where he would die in less than a year?"

Their expression turned to horror and their heads began to bobble and shake.

"No!"

"Cannot imagine why you would ask such a thing!"

"Die? He will probably outlive us all!"

Now it was Miranda's turn to shake. The look of satisfaction on the dowager's face turned to delight as she rose and thanked the doctors. For her own part, the words were just sinking in.

Adrian was not dying, after all.

He had lied to her all along.

Although she could not think of a reason for him to do so, the doctors, by their own admission, had never told him that his condition was so deteriorated that he would die. He had made it up and used it to explain and excuse his actions. To lull her into the situation that now existed—one that he could escape from without difficulty.

She could not breathe.

Cordelia watched all the color drain from Miranda's face as the doctors left. She had gambled and won, and now things would work out the way she'd planned. She did not care why Adrian had lied to Miranda, but it suited her just fine.

She crossed the room and took several of the papers from the package. Holding them out to Miranda, she explained the situation again.

"You will note that the settlement offered if you sign these now is most generous, Miranda."

It took only a few minutes to get the signatures in the correct places on the documents. Although Miranda had not moved from her seat or spoken, Cordelia thought it best to clarify a few of the clauses that she'd just signed.

"You have two days to vacate these premises, Miranda. You are no longer welcome here or on any other Windmere property. And take with you only your personal clothing. Any jewelry or valuables remain with the Windmere estate."

Cordelia gathered up all of the documents and

walked out of the drawing room and called for the Windmere carriage. Climbing in, she was quite pleased with her afternoon's work. Windmere might balk, but Miranda's signature and absence would convince him that this was the right course.

It would be a blustery encounter, but she would prevail…as she just had.

Chapter Twenty

Exhausted from days of traveling to Windmere Park and back again, Adrian walked into his study and poured himself a brandy. Although he would have been happy enough to remain there and wait for Miranda to join him, she had chosen not to come. Now he was here and she was not.

"Where did you say the duchess went?" he asked Sherman when the butler finally entered the room.

"I did not say, Your Grace."

A hint of belligerence permeated the butler's reply, which was odd. Sherman had never been anything but helpful and efficient.

"And if you did say, where would you say she went?" Adrian shook his head, tired from his journey and anxious, very anxious, to see his wife. The week or so before he'd been called away had been troubling to him. Something was wrong between them and he could not identify it. It was not like Miranda to ignore his invitation and especially not reply to it. And he had even invited Lady Allendale to be their guest, hoping it would make her travel more enjoyable.

He looked at Sherman now and lifted his eyebrows, waiting for an answer.

"I could not say, Your Grace."

"Enough of this, man. Just tell me where the duchess is!" His voice raised to shouting, he glared at the servant. Before he could answer, Thompson came running in.

"She is gone, Your Grace!"

"The duchess is gone? I know she is out, but I am trying to discover her location."

"She left, sir. About two days after you did."

"I am exhausted. This exchange might be humorous or even make sense if I was in better shape, but, gentlemen, I have lost my patience."

Walking to the door, he called out, "Fisk!" If no one else could explain this, his wife's maid could and would. When the woman did not come, Adrian ran up the stairs to his wife's rooms. "Fisk!" he called again.

"Your Grace," Sherman said from right behind him. "The duchess left after she had some meeting with the dowager."

"My mother was here?"

"Yes, sir. The dowager sent a note and the duchess accepted her call. It was my impression that the duchess thought you had approved of it."

"I would never have done that, Sherman. You knew that."

He pushed open the door to her dressing room and looked around. As far as he could tell, only a few gowns were not there. "So, when this meeting happened and the duchess left, where did she say she was going?"

"She left no address or indication of her destination, sir."

"And Fisk? Did Fisk go with her?" Her maid would never let her go off alone. She was too loyal.

Adrian searched through the bureau, looking for something to tell him where Miranda might be. He found everything there. Miranda's hair combs, her jewelry, even her wedding ring, and the necklace and earrings he'd given her as an engagement gift. He was beginning to worry now.

"Fisk was let go, sir."

Adrian turned to face them. "Let go? The duchess turned Fisk out?"

"No, sir, the dowager did that. Then she had her man watch as the duchess packed a few of her things, and he followed her out."

"This is bizarre. You are telling me that my mother arrived and met with my wife, then fired my wife's maid and turned Miranda out of her own house with nothing but a few of her gowns?"

The two servants looked at each other and then at him.

"Yes, Your Grace, that is what happened."

Adrian stared at them, trying to figure out his next

step. He'd been gone for nine days, which meant that this had happened a week before. Miranda had been gone for a week and no one in the household knew where she was. He would need some help…and he would need to speak to his mother.

"Sherman, send a footman to see if Lord Parker can be located and brought here. He may be at the club." Adrian began tugging off his travel garments as he walked to his room. "Thompson, we may be on the road again, so please prepare for it."

The last time he'd spoken to his mother, she had mentioned wanting him to divorce his wife. Was that what the meeting was about? Had his mother tried to force Miranda into something?

He took off his shirt and washed his face and hands with the just-delivered hot water. "And find Mr. Anderson and have him come here."

It took less than a half hour for Adrian to discover the absence of his wife, change and be in the carriage heading to the dowager's house. He hoped it would take less time to discuss what she had done and to find Miranda.

"It was her own decision, Windmere. Here are the documents."

"An annulment? You are trying to tell me that Miranda agreed to have our marriage annulled?"

He took the papers from her hands and read them over quickly. In consideration for her cooperation in the annulment proceedings, she would receive a large settlement. The only requirements would be for her to submit to any examinations requested by the courts, and to sign away any claim to Windmere properties, assets or funds.

"Being barren is an extremely difficult thing for a woman to face, Windmere. When she realized the futility of remaining duchess if she could not fulfill her primary responsibility, she agreed to accept the annulment."

"Her primary responsibility was to be my wife, Mother." Adrian dragged his fingers through his hair and fought the urge to commit murder. "What else did you say to her to make her sign this piece of trash?"

"Really, Windmere. I did not force her to do anything," his mother answered. "It was finding out that you'd been lying to her for months about your health and about that woman that convinced her, if anything did."

"That woman? My health? What are you talking about?" Adrian walked to the couch and dropped onto it.

"Your mistress, Mrs. Robinson. Although I am embarrassed that you want me to speak of her with you."

He could swear that she blushed. "Mother, there is nothing we could speak of that would do that to you. What about her?"

"You used to be discreet, Windmere. But your reunion with her and the new house you've bought for her are the talk of the ton. You had to know that Miranda would be told sooner or later."

"For your information, and for that of anyone you care to discuss this with, Mrs. Robinson is not my mistress. She is marrying an American and leaving London within a few weeks. The house I bought is for Miranda."

"You bought a house for her? So you did plan a separation, then?"

The look of glee in his mother's eyes worried him. "I bought the house so that Miranda has a place to live when I die."

"According to the doctors, you will live a long life, Windmere. I think that was the key in Miranda's decision. Once they told her of your true condition and she knew you'd been lying, she signed the papers without asking a question."

He stared in shocked silence at her words. Dare he believe her? "When did you speak to the doctors?"

"I told her that we had discussed a divorce, and she seemed to think that you wouldn't live long enough to go through with it. We summoned Drs. Wilkins, Penworthy and Lloyd and they assured her they never told you that you were dying."

"Brava, Mother! You executed this with the precision of a ballet. Telling each of us just enough of the truth to pull us in and just enough lies to make it work to your advantage."

He turned from her, so furious he could not think clearly. For several moments he paced in front of her. Could he believe her about his condition? He thought back to the incident that had started this whole chain of events in motion. So, they had not been speaking of him after all? How incredibly stupid of him not to realize it!

All of this could have been avoided if he'd only…

But if he'd not thought he was dying, he would never have looked at Miranda differently. He'd never have tried to settle his estates or make arrangements for her. He'd never have gone back to Windmere Park and begun to discover the real Miranda under the layers she'd built to protect herself from the life they led. He'd never have fallen in love with her or made love to her as he had. He would have continued on his path and never realized what he was missing.

Expecting his death had been a stupid mistake, perhaps, but it had caused so many wonderful things to happen to him. And this terrible one. Miranda should not bear the brunt of his stupidity.

"I will find her, Mother, and I will tear up this agreement in front of her."

"Do not be hasty, Windmere."

"Hasty?"

"She has not conceived in over seven years of marriage. This is your chance to wed again. You can marry a young healthy woman who will bear you many children. You have the time, now that you know you aren't going to die."

"I know that this is unheard of, Mother, but I have discovered the problem is not hers. It is not Miranda who is barren, but me. The medications I have been taking for years have most likely caused my infertility."

His mother looked shocked at his admission. But he'd had a frank discussion with several apothecaries and with Mrs. Gresham, and all knew of stories involving the same situation as his.

"So, an annulment is not going to work. And I will not testify to anything other than the truth about this. Would you like me to tell the courts that the Duke of Windmere cannot produce a child?"

Horror filled her face and she shook her head. "You must be mistaken in this. A new bride, a new wife, and you'll see that it was Miranda's fault."

That was when the truth hit him. His mother had planned this to rid herself of Miranda, who was beginning to be her own person, and to put into her place another woman who would be under her control. "Before I make any decisions, do you have someone in mind?" he asked.

"There would be many suitable candidates, Windmere. One I can think of immediately is—"

"Miss Stevenson?" he finished for her.

"Yes. She is attractive, well mannered, young enough to be guided in marriage by an older, more experienced husband. Juliet is also one of five sisters and three brothers, so has a much better family history than… some others may have."

"And she and Lord Parker have reached an understanding, and their engagement will be announced by her parents shortly."

"Never say that!" The dowager looked stricken by the news, and Adrian almost enjoyed it. "You have the higher precedence, your titles are older and more powerful, you have more estates and wealth. How could she consider him when you are a more advantageous match for her, or for any woman?"

"For two reasons, Mother. One—she is in love with Parker and two—I am already married and plan to stay that way."

"I will not let you interfere with this, Windmere."

He walked over until he stood above her, leaning close so she could hear his whispered words.

"If you ever step foot on to any Windmere property other than this one or your dower cottage at Windmere Park, I will have you escorted off. If you attempt to contact me or Miranda, except to offer your felicitations in writing on the birth of any child we might have, I will cut your allowance in half. If you do anything to interfere in our lives again, or even if I *suspect* that you are, I will change my will and take out every personal arrangement I have made for your upkeep and care in the event you survive me."

He paused and remembered one other thing, something that had allowed her to wreak havoc in their lives—too much information. "I have discovered two of those in my employ who were loyal to you and who provided you with what you needed to hurt my wife. I will root out the rest and turn them out without hesitation."

"Windmere," she whispered as he turned to leave. "I am your mother."

"Ah, but she is my wife and I love her."

He thought he heard her gasp, but he would not turn

around again. Adrian left his mother's house for what
he hoped and planned would be the last time.

He spent the next four weeks searching for her. His
attempts to speak to Lady Allendale were deflected for
more than a week before he discovered Miranda's friend
had left town. Lord Allendale would not reveal his
wife's whereabouts or plans, so Adrian was stymied
there. Runners hired to search went to the places at
which they'd stayed in Bath and Bristol and Brighton,
but could find no sign of her. Other than Lady Allendale, Adrian knew of no other friends in town in whom
she would confide.

He summoned the doctors and confirmed that his
mother had told him the truth. They had been speaking
outside his window about someone else, and that person had passed away a month before. Adrian was grateful that they were not discussing him and hopeful that
they were actually more knowledgeable than he'd given
them credit for being.

Parker was so outraged when Adrian told him of the
dowager's plans for Miss Stevenson that he went immediately to her parents and made his offer of marriage.
Now free of the death sentence that had hung over him
for months, Adrian convinced Will to wait until everything had been resolved with Miranda so that they could
stand as witnesses at the wedding.

The house that he had lovingly picked out and fur-
nished for Miranda stood finished and ready for an oc-

cupant. It was funny, in a strange way, how he had made it so personally hers, and she did not need it.

But then again, she might want it.

He would not force her to stay married to him. His solicitor examined the agreement that she'd signed and said it was both legal and binding if she chose to let it stand. If she decided that Adrian was not worth the pain and trouble he'd caused her, he would not only pay her the settlement agreed in the document, but he had an amount equal to half her dowry set aside for her use, as well. And if she allowed the money to be handled by his managers, he knew it would increase over the years.

But first he needed to find her.

With September upon them and most of the ton leaving for their country estates and the hunting and harvest season, he was faced with the reality that she might truly have disappeared from his life. His heart hurt whenever he thought of her alone somewhere. And he knew he must find her.

He closed up both Warfield Place and Miranda's house, as he called it now, and headed for Windmere Park. Leaving behind a small staff in case she should return, he left messages for her with the Allendales and traveled north. Parker promised to visit as soon as possible, and said he looked forward to teaching Miss Stevenson how to play billiards.

Adrian's breathing worsened as it always did in the autumn, but now he did not fear it as more than it was—the change of seasons. Mrs. Gresham still visited him and continued to offer advice and tonics to help him. Now that Miranda was gone, he went back on to the regimen that seemed to help him the most. If she returned to him and wanted to try to conceive a child, he would stop taking the ingredients that Mrs. Gresham identified as possible causes of infertility.

When the trees grew bare and the days began with frost covering the hills, he finally received a note from Parker that gave him a glimmer of hope. Miss Stevenson had received a letter from the viscountess that told of her arrival at their northern estate. The Allendales lived only twenty miles from Windmere Park.

Lady Allendale was the only person who Miranda would contact. She was his only hope in finding his wife. So, deciding that she would evade him if she knew of his approach, Adrian did the unthinkably rude thing of showing up in Allendale without an invitation and without warning of his arrival.

Chapter Twenty-One

$\infty\!\!\infty\!\!\infty\!\!\infty$

"Lady Allendale! How good of you to finally join me."

He'd been kept waiting for three hours and forty minutes, an unheard of delay for a guest, even an unannounced, uninvited one whom a hostess hated. Adrian forced the smile to stay on his face as she curtsied before him. He nearly reached out to help her back to her feet when her pregnant form made rising tricky, but he changed his mind, enjoying her difficulty immensely for the moment or two it lasted.

"Your Grace, how kind of you to visit…so unexpectedly. Have you had some tea? Or would you prefer coffee?"

He had not wasted time on drinking tea. He had opened the door to the hallway and taken up a position where he could see both the stairs and the corridor. Although he didn't expect that she would carry the message herself, he did suspect that one would be sent...to wherever Miranda was staying.

"No, thank you, Lady Allendale. I came simply to ask you a few questions and promise not to keep you from your busy schedule." He waited for her to be seated and then met her gaze. The hatred there did not surprise him in the least. "Where is she?"

"She, Your Grace? Whomever do you mean?"

She was going to make this as hard as she could, he saw. "My wife, of course."

"Ah, but Your Grace, according to the documents I saw, you no longer have a wife," she said, with a lethal smile. "Fortunate, wouldn't you say, for a man who does not want one?"

He sighed. She would fight him every step of the way. This could take days of not-so-polite repartee before he found her, and that was if the lady had not sent word already.

"I am not her enemy, Lady Allendale. I need to find her and make things right between us."

"Perhaps this is the right way? Perhaps she is happier not being your wife?" The viscountess stood and approached where he stood. "Perhaps you should go home and find yourself a new wife, as your mother planned?"

"I will grovel at her feet, Lady, but not at yours. Tell me where she is."

"And what will you threaten her with, Your Grace? What else can you take from her now that she's lost her dignity, her standing in society, her husband, the only family she has known for eight years and every possession she ever had?"

"I do not have anything to threaten her with, for she holds all the power in her hands. If she wishes me to leave without her, I will, once I have the chance to speak to her. If she wishes to rescind the agreement and return to me, I will take her from here. But she once told me that all she ever wanted was a husband who loved her. I am that husband. I simply want the chance to prove it to her."

Sophie's expression was still hard and he did not think she would relent in this. As much as it frustrated him, he was also pleased that she was such a fierce defender of her friend.

"There is a small guest house next to the lake on the south side of the property. She lives there."

Adrian turned around to face Lord Allendale.

"Oh, John! Why did you tell him?" Lady Allendale cried.

"Because, my love, you were about to call him out and I did not want his blood on the new Aubusson."

"My thanks, Lord Allendale."

"Allendale, please," he said, shaking the hand Adrian offered. "I will let my wife have a go at you if you force her friend in any way, Your Grace. I must consider my wife's delicate condition and all."

Nodding and anxious to go, Adrian noted the directions Allendale gave him, a shortcut that would lead him to the cottage. He tried to slow his pace, but soon he was running down the path to the lake and along the shore to the left. He was about to enter the house when he saw her sitting near the water. Waiting to catch his breath, he approached quietly, not wanting to frighten her. He was a few steps away when he realized she was asleep.

Adrian sat on the grass and, as he had so many times before, watched her sleep. The chair on which she sat was in the shade, so the sun did not beat directly down on her. A breeze teased some loose strands of her hair and his hands itched to feel it, just as his mouth craved a taste of hers. It had been a month since last he'd seen her, and she'd changed somehow.

Miranda stirred as though she was aware of his presence, but he waited silently for her to wake. She shifted in the chair and then opened her eyes, blinking to clear her vision when she saw him. Adrian guessed she probably thought he was a dream.

It hurt so much more than she ever thought possible to see him again—the face, the eyes, the body and soul of the man she loved so much that she would leave him behind rather than stand in his way. She had convinced herself that enough time had passed, and that she would be able to have a polite conversation with him when he did finally arrive. She'd known it was only a matter of time, and now he was here.

"Your Grace," she said, struggling to her feet.

"I thought we were far past that, Miranda."

He looked as though he wanted to say something but

could not find the words. She knew the feeling exactly, for she suffered from it, too.

Adrian gazed out over the lake's smooth surface as though searching for a way to begin. But begin what?

"My father's death was considered by some to be quite fortuitous in its timing," he said in a low voice. "By the time death freed him from his debauched and wastrel ways, he'd lost or mortgaged most of everything associated with the Windmere titles. My brother was overwhelmed at the near-destruction to our fortunes and estates." He turned and looked at her with such a bleak expression that it hurt her to see it.

"I know that your father had hopes of marrying you to him, but my mother would not consider you for the new duke. You understand that part, do you not?" He raised his eyebrow and nodded when she did.

This was no surprise to her, her blood and ancestry was not close to being considered acceptable to marry a duke, especially not one as high in standing as the Duke of Windmere. He rubbed his hands over his face and turned away again. Part of her wanted to go to him, but she knew that she needed to hear his explanation first.

"Your dowry saved us, Miranda. It saved the lands and the people from complete ruin. My brother's untimely death within days of our marriage was an ironic twist of fate for it placed you where no one believed you should be and yet where you truly deserved to be…Duchess of Windmere." Turning now and meeting her gaze, he continued. "The shock of it, his death and inheriting the title, were almost overwhelming. I was not prepared to be the duke and then I was. I fear that I relied too much on…the dowager's advice and direction, but I confess that I knew no other way at the time. I simply knew I needed to be what my father had failed to be and my brother had not had the time to be."

Then, like a dam bursting from too much pressure, he fell to his knees before her and wrapped his arms around her.

"I am sorry, Miranda. Sorry for the pain I've caused you. Sorry for the years we lost because of my stupidity and my need to be someone I was not, nor ever could be. Sorry for turning your life into a hell and never realizing it."

She could not stop the tears that fell freely now. And he could not stop the words.

"I am sorry for lying to you over and over, so many times that I've lost count. I am sorry for not valuing you as the gift you were to me, until it was too late. And I am sorry for not being there to protect you when you most needed me."

He was silent then, just holding her, and she knew he was unable to say anything more. She touched his hair and stroked his neck. Adrian looked up at her then and she saw the tears in his eyes.

"If you want the annulment, I will not stop it. I will say whatever needs to be said, but you must know that our problems in having a child are mine, not yours. You must not take the blame for this. And I will provide for you regardless of what you decide."

He climbed to his feet, took her shoulders and pulled her closer. She thought he might kiss her, but he continued to explain. "But I do not want our marriage to end. I know now that I was wrong about my condition and that I won't die. When I found out, all I could think of was spending the rest of my days with you. Please, Miranda, come back to me and let me prove how much I love you? Give me the chance to give you the kind of marriage you said you wanted?"

She watched him as he spilled out his heart and soul to her. There was so much to straighten out, so much to tell him, but he had just offered her the very thing she had always wanted with him—a marriage based on love. How could she say no to that? Especially now—now that she could give him the thing he needed most.

"Adrian," she said, stepping closer. "All I wanted was a true marriage. And your love. I never married the duke, I married the man."

"If you come back to me, we can make it work. You can be the duchess or just my wife."

"Do I need to see your mother?"

"No, I've disowned her."

"Adrian, you cannot disown your mother."

"I wish I could lay the blame at her feet and say it was all her manipulations. But it was my dishonesty that made us vulnerable to it. Parker told me countless times to tell you the truth—well, at least what I thought was the truth. But I thought I could make your decisions for you."

She needed to know a few things right away. She suspected that once she gave him her answer there would not be much talking.

"You really thought you were dying?"

"I did. I overheard the doctors discussing 'the poor man' right after they'd examined me, and I was convinced it was me. The symptoms and situation were so much like mine that, in a panic, I believed them."

"Did you discuss divorce with your mother?"

He stepped back and shook his head. "To say that she discussed it would be putting too fine a head on it. She seemed to have this idea and then hired investigators to find some evidence to be used. Unfortunately, it would seem that I provided that to her as well."

"The men? The introductions? What ever were you thinking? I found your list on your desk, with names and amounts of money and notations of times I'd met them and all."

"I should probably move away so you cannot do me bodily harm when I tell you." He did take a step back. "I am not certain that Lady Allendale will come to my rescue."

Miranda looked over her shoulder and saw that both Sophie and her husband were watching from a discreet distance. She waved to let them know she was fine, and then turned back to hear his explanation.

"When I thought I was dying, I discovered that our

marriage settlement provided you with almost nothing if I died without an heir. The first thing I did was try to produce one with you."

"Ah, the additional attentions."

"Just so. I also decided to set up some kind of financial arrangements and even bought a house for you so that you could live off of the estate if you wanted."

"The house? The one on Charleston Street?"

"You know of it? Truly? My mother said you did, but I was not certain when she was lying and when she told the truth."

"I found about it and even saw you there, with Mrs. Robinson."

"When? We were only there once, when I asked her opinion of the best time to tell you about it. I thought to wait until I had some sign of my impending death, though Parker argued with me to tell you so you would not worry."

She sat down and laughed for a moment. "It is my house?" Now it made sense to her, especially knowing that her favorite painting hung on a wall inside it. "And the men?"

"Ah, the men. In my plan to take care of you, I realized you wanted more from a marriage than just a house and an income. You wanted a husband, and so I set out to find you one."

"You were looking for a husband for me?"

"Oh, Miranda," he said, taking her hand in his. "I did

not want to, but I was so in love with you that I tried to make arrangements for everything you'd want and need once I was gone."

"And apparently you did a thorough job of it. Had you introduced me to all the prospective husbands you'd chosen or were there still more?"

"I was simply trying to do the best for you."

She could see the love shining in his eyes and knew the truth of his story. She reached up and brought his mouth down to hers so that she could kiss him. Touching his face, she smiled.

"I do understand what I have put you through, Miranda, and I want you to make the decision about this. I just needed the chance to tell you everything before you disappeared from my life forever."

"I was not going to disappear, Adrian. I just needed some time to recover from all that had happened before seeking you out. Sophie has been able to glean some of what you've told me from various people she knows, but I could not face any of this or you until I felt stronger."

"And now? Will you at least promise to stay here so that I know you are being cared for?"

"Actually, I am ready to come home with you. Sophie asked me to remain for her confinement, but Mrs. James said there's a reason women who have not yet had children should avoid it."

"Is Mrs. James here, then? Is Lady Allendale due to give birth soon?"

"Mrs. James arrived a few weeks ago and will come back in late December for the birth."

"And what was the reason she gave to you for not attending?"

"She said it would be too scary for me when it was time to have my own, if I watched the viscountess go through it. Apparently Sophie is not the best of patients."

He laughed—a sound so precious to her. She had missed so many things about him in the last months. His laughter, his humor, his loving. At least now she could give him the one thing he wanted most, but had not asked her about yet.

"If you will allow it, Mrs. James will stay with us in the spring…? I would rather have her in attendance than Dr. Blake."

He opened his mouth to speak, but could only stutter and stammer, unable to say anything. She lifted his hand to her belly and let him feel the evidence of the new life growing inside of her. His eyes widened and then he just smiled. A few minutes passed before he managed to clear his throat and speak.

"And I thought you were so impressed by Dr. Blake. After all, he has written a book on the subject." He kissed her then, long and deep, and she prayed he would not stop. "Be my wife, Miranda?"

"Only if you stop looking for husbands for me," she said.

"There is and shall be only one husband for you, Your Grace. And he is here to take you home."

* * *

"When Sophie described this to me, I simply had no understanding of it."

They lay together in his bed at Windmere Park and she knew they would not be leaving his chambers anytime soon. Once she had explained about the strange occurrences that a woman "in a delicate condition" experienced, he wanted proof. So in the middle of the night, when the urge came upon her, she sent him in search of the items needed.

"And now?" he asked. "What order is it this time?"

"You. No, the clotted cream..." She paused and shook her head. Tasting the melted chocolate on her fingers, she nodded. "You with the chocolate and clotted cream."

He laughed and licked her fingers clean, sending all sorts of wonderful sensations through her body. And when he sucked them into his mouth and teased them with his tongue and teeth, she wanted him to do that to other places, too.

"And when do we get to *my* urgings and cravings?" he asked.

Before she could answer, he provided his own. He bent over and took her breast in his mouth. Adrian stopped for a moment, took a handful of the clotted cream from the bowl he'd brought into bed and smeared it on her breasts and belly and other places.

"This could work. I could get to like you in this delicate condition if you promise to continue with these urgings—" he licked from one nipple to the other "—and cravings." He kissed a path down her belly and between her thighs. Soon she could not remember which craving belonged to whom. She did discover that he liked the chocolate even more than the cream, and that she liked it in whichever order he wanted.

And the Duke of Windmere proved to his duchess that night why she needed only one husband in her life.

Epilogue

"What name do you give this child?" Reverend Grayson's voice intoned deeply. A shiver traveled down Miranda's spine as she watched this momentous occasion from her place in the family pew.

"Alexander Thomas Geoffrey Warfield." Smiling, the Earl of Harbridge and the Duke of Sommerfield, his godfathers, answered together.

The rector took the child from his godmother's arms and, holding the still-sleeping infant over the font, poured a measure of the baptismal water over his head. Alex stirred, but did not cry out, pleasing Miranda in some newly-acquired motherly fashion. Then, as the cold water spilled over his head, his hardy cry echoed through the church and evoked the knowing smiles and sighs of those attending.

The one that lit her husband's face was nothing subtle. Adrian laughed loudly at the disgruntled look on his son's face. That they had reached this place in their lives was still a miracle to both of them, something they cherished and enjoyed every moment they could.

Miranda stood with the rest of the congregation to hear the minister's final words declaring her son to be part of the community and exhorting them to guide him during his life. Then, a bit sooner than might be considered seemly, Adrian lifted the baby from the arms of the minister and held him close, drying his head with a piece of linen and soothing him in a hushed whisper of a voice. That brought additional smiles and sighs as more than one person near her commented on the duke's obvious affection for his son…and heir. The one person who did not react was the dowager who sat stiff and silent at Miranda's side.

In spite of his strident and loud objections, Adrian had finally relented and allowed Miranda to invite his mother to the ceremony. The dowager had accepted the invitation because to do otherwise would have been both impolite and imprudent considering who held her purse strings. But Miranda did not fool herself into thinking that her presence meant anything more than that. And, if she were honest with her own feelings on the matter, Miranda was not ready for anything more than that.

The final words were spoken and Adrian carried their son to her, placing the squirming bundle into her open arms. With her gentle rocking, the babe quieted and they left the church to return to a breakfast at Windmere House.

"I think the marquess handled himself admirably well through that," Adrian said as they settled into the coach seat with the baby's nurse across from them.

"His good breeding is evident even at this early age," she replied.

Adrian burst out laughing and she joined him. "That is one perspective on it." He reached over and touched the babe's cheek. "Perhaps he was sated and warm and comfortable and only protested when roused from that state."

Just when she began to chuckle, he met her gaze and she saw the fire within his eyes. "I know that if I were sated and warm and in your arms, I would protest any interruption," he whispered in her ear so that the nurse did not hear his words.

Miranda felt the heat creep up into her cheeks as he now touched her lips with the tip of his finger. They had not yet resumed all of their marital activities, but it did not stop them from wanting to. Mrs. James had suggested that she needed a few more weeks to completely heal from the birth of her son and so they would wait before they joined. But Adrian's impertinent comment referred to the marital activities that they had resumed…just last evening.

"Nor would I, Your Grace."

She glanced at the young woman who was doing her best to ignore the personal behavior going on between her employers. From the brightness of her eyes, Miranda knew Adrian's words had been overheard. Well, this was certainly not the first time they had been so obvious in her presence and Miranda knew there would be many more times if Clarissa remained to care for their son.

"Later then, Your Grace?" he asked in the seductive whisper that promised so much pleasure.

"As you wish." She pressed a brief kiss on his mouth and then leaned away. Her body had responded to his invitation and she needed some space to gain control before they arrived back at the house and she needed to be the duchess again.

"Are you pleased with your son?"

"As much as I am pleased that you gave him to me." He lifted her hand to his lips and kissed her hand. "As much as it pleases me that you are my wife…" He kissed her hand again. "As much as it pleases me that you are my duchess." This time he slid his fingers between hers and clasped her hand in his.

The coach arrived at the house and servants stood ready to assist them and their guests. Adrian motioned for the nurse to step out first and then handed the baby out to her. When she thought he would offer his hand to her, Adrian surprised her by pulling the door of the coach closed behind him and taking her into his arms. When she was breathless from his kisses, he released her and watched her reaction.

"What was that for?" she asked as she replaced the wisps of hair dislodged by his ardent attentions. He rearranged his trousers so she knew he was just as affected by it.

"To remind you that you will only need one husband and that I am he."

"I only ever wanted one husband. Truth be told, I have only ever wanted you to be that man," she said, her throat tightening with the emotion she felt in her heart for him.

"Now that we agree on that, shall we go in for breakfast with our guests?" Adrian turned the knob and pushed the door of the carriage open. "Cook told me of a new chocolate concoction that she is presenting for the first time in honor of Alexander's christening."

"Chocolate?" Miranda asked, smiling at his obvious temptation. "I like chocolate." She could not help how her voice grew husky just thinking about him…and chocolate.

"Cook promises to reserve a portion of it for us to enjoy in private," he said holding out his hand to assist her from the coach.

"Well, Your Grace," she said, smoothing her dress as she stood at his side, "I suppose the sooner we begin this, the sooner it ends."

Her attempts to remain unmoved and to retain her sense of dignity failed and she broke out laughing at his expression as he realized just how much longer they would have to endure the company of others.

"If we hurry?" he asked.

"If we sneak away," she offered, as he tugged her along, hurrying them and their guests into the house to begin their meal.

And, if the Duke and Duchess of Windmere seemed to hurry a bit or if they could not be found for a brief time later in the morning, their friends knowingly smiled over their eccentric personal ways and continued to celebrate the birth of the new heir to the Warfield family fortune, titles and estates until the couple returned.

* * * * *

Harlequin Historicals®
Historical Romantic Adventure!

PICK UP A HARLEQUIN HISTORICALS BOOK AND DISCOVER EXCITING AND EMOTIONAL LOVE STORIES SET IN THE AMERICAN LANDSCAPE!

ON SALE JUNE 2005

SPRING BRIDES
by Stacy/Reavis/Crooks

Fall in love this spring with three brand-new stories of romance: In *Three Brides and a Wedding Dress*, a mail-order bride arrives in town expecting one groom, but ends up falling for his cousin instead! An Eastern miss discovers love can be wonderful—and complicated—in the harsh Wyoming wilderness, in *The Winter Heart*. And in *McCord's Destiny*, a female architect gets the offer of a lifetime from a man who once stole her heart—and wishes to steal it again.

HEART OF THE STORM
by Mary Burton

Lighthouse keeper Ben Mitchell rescues a beautiful woman when a ship sinks off the Carolina coast. While helping her recuperate, he is fascinated by the mysterious Rachel Emmons. She won't reveal her past, will only live for the present. Can Ben uncover her secrets before he loses his heart to her completely?

www.eHarlequin.com

HHWEST39

Harlequin Historicals®
Historical Romantic Adventure!

SAVOR THESE STIRRING TALES OF LOVE IN REGENCY ENGLAND FROM HARLEQUIN HISTORICALS

ON SALE MAY 2005

THE DUCHESS'S NEXT HUSBAND
by Terri Brisbin

The Duke of Windmere receives word that he's going to die, and tries to get his affairs in order—which includes finding his wife a new husband! But as the duke's efforts go awry and he starts to fall in love with the duchess again, dare he hope they will find true happiness together—before it's too late?

THE MISSING HEIR
by Gail Ranstrom

Presumed dead, Adam Hawthorne returns to London after four years to discover his uncle passed away and the young widow is in possession of his inheritance. Adam is determined to uncover the truth, but the closer he gets to Grace Forbush, the more he desires his beautiful aunt-by-marriage—in his arms!

www.eHarlequin.com

HHMED43

Harlequin Historicals®
Historical Romantic Adventure!

PICK UP A HARLEQUIN HISTORICALS BOOK AND DISCOVER EXCITING AND EMOTIONAL LOVE STORIES SET IN THE OLD WEST!

ON SALE MAY 2005

ROCKY MOUNTAIN MAN
by Jillian Hart

On the edge of a small Montana town, ex-convict Duncan Hennessey lives a solitary life. When widow Betsy Hunter delivers his laundry, he saves her from a bear attack. Will this lonely beast of a man fall for the sweet beauty—or keep her at arm's length forever?

HER DEAREST ENEMY
by Elizabeth Lane

Brandon Calhoun, the richest man in town, wants to break up the romance of his daughter and the brother of town spinster Harriet Smith. He needs Harriet's help. But the feisty schoolteacher won't agree. Can the handsome banker charm her into his scheme—and into his life?

www.eHarlequin.com

HHWEST38

If you enjoyed what you just read,
then we've got an offer you can't resist!

Take 2 bestselling
love stories FREE!

Plus get a FREE surprise gift!

Clip this page and mail it to Harlequin Reader Service®

IN U.S.A.	**IN CANADA**
3010 Walden Ave.	P.O. Box 609
P.O. Box 1867	Fort Erie, Ontario
Buffalo, N.Y. 14240-1867	L2A 5X3

YES! Please send me 2 free Harlequin Historicals® novels and my free surprise gift. After receiving them, if I don't wish to receive anymore, I can return the shipping statement marked cancel. If I don't cancel, I will receive 6 brand-new novels every month, before they're available in stores! In the U.S.A., bill me at the bargain price of $4.69 plus 25¢ shipping and handling per book and applicable sales tax, if any*. In Canada, bill me at the bargain price of $5.24 plus 25¢ shipping and handling per book and applicable taxes**. That's the complete price and a savings of over 10% off the cover prices—what a great deal! I understand that accepting the 2 free books and gift places me under no obligation ever to buy any books. I can always return a shipment and cancel at any time. Even if I never buy another book from Harlequin, the 2 free books and gift are mine to keep forever.

246 HDN DZ7Q
349 HDN DZ7R

Name	(PLEASE PRINT)
Address	Apt.#
City	State/Prov.	Zip/Postal Code

Not valid to current Harlequin Historicals® subscribers.

Want to try two free books from another series?
Call 1-800-873-8635 or visit www.morefreebooks.com.

* Terms and prices subject to change without notice. Sales tax applicable in N.Y.
** Canadian residents will be charged applicable provincial taxes and GST.
All orders subject to approval. Offer limited to one per household.
® are registered trademarks owned and used by the trademark owner and or its licensee.

HIST04R   ©2004 Harlequin Enterprises Limited

eHARLEQUIN.com
The Ultimate Destination for Women's Fiction

Calling all aspiring writers!
Learn to craft the perfect romance novel
with our useful tips and tools:

- Take advantage of our **Romance Novel Critique Service** for detailed advice from romance professionals.

- Use our **message boards** to connect with writers, published authors and editors.

- Enter our **Writing Round Robin—** you could be published online!

- Learn many tools of the writer's trade from editors and authors in our **On Writing** section!

- **Writing guidelines** for Harlequin or Silhouette novels—what our editors *really* look for.

**Learn more about romance writing
from the experts—
visit www.eHarlequin.com today!**

INTLTW04

Harlequin Historicals®
Historical Romantic Adventure!

SAVOR THE BREATHTAKING ROMANCES AND THRILLING ADVENTURES OF HARLEQUIN HISTORICALS

ON SALE JUNE 2005

THE VISCOUNT'S BRIDE
by Ann Elizabeth Cree

Faced with her guardian's unsavory choice of a husband or the love of a sensible man, Lady Chloe Daventry decides on a sensible match. But she hadn't counted on the dashing Brandt, Lord Salcombe, thwarting her careful plans!

MY LADY'S FAVOR
by Joanne Rock

Elysia Rougemont is commanded to marry an aging noble her overlord has chosen for her. When her groom dies on their wedding day, his nephew, Conon St. Simeon, suspects his beautiful aunt-by-marriage had a hand in his demise. Can Elysia convince Conon she's innocent of wrongdoing—and guilty of loving him?

www.eHarlequin.com

HHMED44

HQN™

We *are* romance™

The earl was a beast—and she was his salvation.
New York Times bestselling author

SHANNON DRAKE

The mask he wears is said to hide a face too horrific to behold,
yet the earl hides another secret—he is searching for the truth
behind the mysterious death of his parents. Beautiful Egyptologist
Camille Montgomery is his key to unlocking the secret—
by posing as his fiancée! But there is more at stake than
simply a masquerade….

"A deft mix of history, romance and suspense."—*Publishers Weekly*

Wicked

The newest release by acclaimed author Shannon Drake,
available in April.

www.HQNBooks.com

PHSD033